BILLY'S BROTHER

BILLY'S BROTHER

KENNETH MARTIN

Billy's Brother takes place next year in San Francisco. Readers familiar with the City during the epidemic will recognize the names of certain institutions and public figures. In all other respects this is a work of fiction. No resemblance to actual persons living or dead is intended, nor should it be inferred.

First published June 1989 by
GMP Publishers Ltd,
PO Box 247, London N17 9QR

World Copyright © Kenneth Martin

Distributed in North America by
Alyson Publications Inc.,
40 Plympton St, Boston, MA 02118, USA

British Library Cataloguing in Publication Data
Martin, Kenneth, *1939-*
 Billy's Brother.
 I. Title
 823'.914 [F]

ISBN 0-85449-109-0

Printed and bound in the European Community by
Norhaven A/S, Viborg, Denmark

I saw a rainbow bird the night I buried Billy's ashes. One night after work I forced myself to take the ashes up the bare rocky hill above the Castro to bury them among the poppies – I'd read about a man who planted poppy seeds on Corona Heights in memory of those who'd died. Some of the rocks sticking out of the rubble and stunted yellow grass resembled headstones, but I found no flowers in the stony ground.

The upper air shifted with the fog that slid in from the ocean every night like an indifferent ghost; the buildings below looked soaked and battered through the blurry haunted drizzle. For a moment the mist thinned, and across from me I saw a gigantic bird, its wingspan 12 or 15 feet, hovering over the toy people heading home from work. The broad colored stripes on its paper wings glowed and flared in the darkening air, soaking up all the light there was: red, orange, yellow, green, blue and purple, the brilliant colors of the life that Billy chose to live until he died.

Chapter One

ON MONDAY AFTERNOON I ran on East River Road towards St. Paul. Even that close to midday the sun cast long shadows of trees on the snow in the parks and gardens above the steep river banks. The ground underfoot was cruelly hard and treacherous, and the Mississippi was still frozen, but it looked to me as if the dark strip of thin ice edging the bottom of the bank far down on my right got wider each day I remembered to look at it.

When I got back to the small wooden house where I was born I lingered on the porch, pretending to wipe the black water off my running shoes while I watched the long street of similar houses with snow in their yards and empty gardens. All I had to do for the rest of the day was rent a movie or skim one of the law journals they still sent me. You could wait a long time on that street for signs of life. Years ago it had been a neighbor, emerging from secrecy for the few moments it took to dump the garbage, who'd heard the screams of two children and called the police.

Inside the message light was flashing on the machine. One flash, one message. One was an event, two aroused all kinds of expectations.

"This is Billy," my brother said on the tape. "I'm very sick." I froze: I could hardly hear, let alone recognize the voice, which sounded artificial, pushed by an act of will from a body that had stopped helping him. "Come to General Hospital."

I panicked. Where was he now?

"In San Francisco," Billy said after a pause. He sounded as if he was almost laughing at me, as if he'd known the incomplete message would cause me to panic. We knew how we'd neglected to stay in touch for 25 years.

I caught a Northwest flight at 6:55. It arrived almost on time. There was nobody to ask for help at the front desk in the deserted lobby at the hospital. An angry intern I forced to stop suggested ICU to get rid of me. The clock said 9:35 as I hopped around waiting for an elevator.

Billy had died ten minutes before I arrived. His face against my hand was already chilling.

I thought: Now I have nothing left. I'm old and tired. Now I want to die too.

Billy's head was bandaged down to his eyebrows, and there were bandages on his right arm and shoulder. The blue-and-white hospital gown, thin as a rag, had come untied at the back and the length of it was twisted around his shoulders. I saw what looked like burn marks on the transparent skin that clung to his right side. His beard and the hair on his chest were nearly white. He looked old and young. He'd aged shockingly each time I saw him every three or four years; I'd used Billy getting older to note that I must be aging too. I didn't feel my age for a long time, because I was hardly ever present for my life. But however thin Billy got, or ravaged from drugs and the kinds of interior journeys he never told me about, he always shone for me with an optimistic smiling light, an air of starting out again and getting it right this time. Patches of the skin on his dead face still looked smooth and shiny. I thought that the cuts and scratches on his cheeks and nose were going to heal nicely. At the same time it was clear to me that wherever Billy was, he wasn't here in this hastily mended body.

Chapter Two

"HE WAS ONLY conscious about an hour," the doctor said, and then he tried to console me. "That must have been when he called you."

"Was it AIDS?"

The doctor stared at me.

"I knew my brother was gay," I said.

"There were no obvious signs of AIDS diseases," he said, "although we can't be sure until there's an autopsy." He rifled back and forth through a hospital chart without once looking down at the pages. "We know your brother was AIDS antibody positive, but so are half the gay men in the city."

I thought: Including you, I'd guess.

"Your brother was thrown or fell from a car on the freeway two miles from here on Friday night," the doctor recited from memory. "He had severe head injuries, and large amounts of alcohol and drugs contributed to the neurological impairment." With an apologetic face: "He'd been admitted to ICU in drug-induced comas on two earlier occasions."

"Somebody tried to kill him or left him to die," I said.

"It looks like that. The police want to talk to you."

"How did he get the burn marks on his skin?" I asked.

"Those were abrasions caused by his body skidding over the ground until his head crashed into the barrier," the doctor said. "Which is why the police think he was thrown forcibly. If he'd fallen his body would probably have come to a halt sooner."

"Oh Jesus," I said.

"Are you alone?"

"Yeah, but I'm okay." He looked dubious. "I guess I'm going to stay in Billy's apartment. Did he have keys on him?"

He'd had keys and a wallet, which the hospital released to me. They told me he'd been wearing sneakers and a pair of jeans and a T-shirt, all of which the police had taken. I wanted to hold on to him. I went back to say goodbye to him again, but when I sat down and looked at his face I knew right away it was useless, he'd left me forever. The only reason I stayed in the room any longer was that I'd just come in again and I didn't want the hospital staff to think I didn't know what I was doing. I looked around for pieces of Billy's life that I could take with me. I looked for something to tell me what to do. There was nothing. But I noticed you could see the freeway from his window, floating in feverish light beyond a small courtyard with a palm tree and a wire fence. Apart from the palm it could have been a Minneapolis suburb, one of the poor ones.

I took a taxi through grubby streets where it surprised me to see so many people walking, and so many of them blacks or Hispanics. I did a double take when I noticed the blooming plants and glossy bushes outside front doors: I caught myself thinking I'd taken a plane trip to another country. It was a short ride, $6 plus tip. The outside of Billy's house looked filthy, with plastic garbage bins to the right of the four steps leading up to two front doors, both with full-length glass panels with cloth pasted over the insides. There was a hand-printed sign taped to the inside of the glass in front of the plastic lace on Billy's door: "Bell not working. Knock loudly."

I had trouble with the three locks. When I finally stepped inside, sweating, I heard a regular slow hammering noise above me. The shadow of a cat that had come to greet its owner squawked and turned its back on me and labored up a dark flight of stairs to the left. The twelve square feet of hallway were littered with mail. Nothing happened when I flicked the light switch next to the door. I gathered the mail into a pile, stuff falling out of envelopes, and climbed the stairs in the dark with my garment bag and a duffle bag and the pile of mail, trying not to drop anything.

The steep stairs turned left at the top, and another short flight led to a hallway running the length of the apartment. The light from the city sky showed two large rooms, quite empty, at this end of the hall. One room didn't have a door; the door to the other was badly hung and banging in a draft I couldn't feel. I found a light above a long strip of mirror in the hall, and then I saw that the mail I held had been ripped open, some of the envelopes and their contents torn down the middle.

At the other end of the hall there was a bedroom with an archway to the left into a large living room and another archway into a large kitchen. I'd seen apartments in bad neighborhoods in Manhattan that cost $2,000 a month for this amount of space. I was stepping on papers on the living room floor. I turned on a lamp and immediately checked to see if there was a window open. The corner of a window sash had come apart and was separated from the glass, but not enough to cause this mess. Books had been dumped on the floor and records emptied from their sleeves.

The cat squawked again. He was a big black comfortable cat and he was sitting by a double food bowl in the kitchen, glaring at me with indignant green eyes. As I moved towards him he edged away, but he kept glancing from his bowls to me and back. The bowls were empty of food or water. I thought he must have been drinking from the toilet. There were about 20 cans of cat food tumbled on the floor next to the oven, and two can openers above the sink. The cat howled when I picked up one of the cans to open it, but he stayed away from his food and water until I left the kitchen.

The door was still banging. I felt overwhelmed, not knowing what to do first, but I found a towel and jammed the door shut, thinking that I just wanted to go to sleep. But I wanted to wake up in the morning. Someone, an enemy of Billy's, had keys to the apartment. I pictured that enemy, who'd killed my brother, cutting the glass in the front door during the night and sliding the chain free. I was too exhausted to deal with the police. I settled for turning on the lights in the two front rooms and carrying two chairs downstairs and stacking them against the inside of the front door.

When I pulled back the sheets on Billy's bed I found semen

stains and a stack of porno magazines. I didn't expect to find a spare set of sheets in the apartment, and I didn't. "Shit!" I swelled with rage at my feckless selfish brother. I'd been lectured so many times by idiotic TV journalists about how hard AIDS was to catch – while all the time I was thinking, this is a nightmare that has nothing to do with Billy – that I was fairly certain the AIDS virus didn't survive in dried semen that was at least three days old. But how dare he put me at risk, how dare he do any of this to me? I thought a drink would be very nice.

The refrigerator, next to a trash bin which stank, had a half-gallon bottle of White Crown vodka and another half-gallon of Mondavi chablis. No tonic, bottled water or juice or milk. The only food was two green apples and a bag of oranges. I took the wine and gin bottles to the kitchen sink and emptied them, turning my head away to try to avoid the power of the smell. The cat bolted from where he'd been gobbling food. I washed out the bottles with hot water and dumped them in the smelly trash bag, and then I drank two mugs of subtly tainted tap water for a bedtime drink.

It seemed fairly safe to go to bed in my underwear, under the comforter but on top of the sheets. The bed was firm but the pillows were flat and thin. When the cat finally finished eating he came and sat in the doorway, grooming himself noisily, checking on my movements with sideways stares between bouts of frenzied licking. As I lay watching him, because he was the only other living thing in the apartment, the light in the kitchen came on behind him.

I chose not to be afraid. I lay there trying to work out a rational explanation, something to do with time switches, while the kitchen light hummed against the ugly yellow walls and uglier yellow floor. Finally, against my better judgment, I got out of bed. The cat retreated as I headed towards the kitchen. The light switch was circular and I hadn't clicked it off completely, which was why it slid on again by itself.

In the middle of that night I woke up drenched in sweat from a dream of abandonment for which I had myself to blame. I lay fearful and defeated, thinking that this time I'd maybe reached my limits. The sheets under me were soaked. Then I remembered what the captain of the plane had announced, a few hours ago. San Francisco was in the middle of a heat wave unprecedented this century. The temperature yesterday had been over 90 degrees, the hottest March day since records began.

Chapter Three

NEXT MORNING THE cat was sitting in the bedroom doorway again, staring at me, shamelessly calculating what use I'd be to him. When his eyes flicked away I realized I'd been staring back. I felt jittery and pressured even after a dead sleep. My body was as sore and stiff as if I'd been in a fight. The room was hot and airless. I lifted a bamboo blind and saw the sun shining in a light blue sky.

When I got out of bed the cat retreated to his food bowl, which was empty again. I fed him and breakfasted on oranges and the first of a lot of cups of good coffee I drank that day. Billy had managed to sneak a bag of ground French Roast into his food regimen – vegetarian, macrobiotic, whatever it was. I drank the coffee at the rectangular glass-topped walnut table in the living room, a comfortable square-shaped room with a tan sofa, a green and orange futon, a big ficus reaching to the ceiling, and a fireplace with ashes in the grate. I started going through Billy's wallet, though I was really thinking about the mess on the floor. It frightened me.

The wallet contained $9, a California ID card, and a Fast Pass for March. I was having trouble focusing or thinking, and I was watching myself and thinking, "He's probably in shock." I took out my wallet and started lining up the contents on the table to see what was missing from Billy's wallet. He had no credit cards, no health insurance card, no voters registration card, no ATM card, no MCI card, no Worldperks card, no video store membership card. No membership cards of any kind. Neither of us had a driver's license. I had reminders in my wallet I'd scribbled to myself on Post-its, and scraps of paper with first names and phone numbers people had pressed on me at meetings, though I rarely called anyone. Billy's wallet had none of that.

I felt unable to make the effort to work out what was going on. The wooden floor was littered from an obviously desperate search. Letters – mostly utility bills with fillers and bank statements with cancelled checks – had been emptied out of envelopes and the pages separated and dumped. Magazines and gay newspapers, *The Advocate* , the *Bay Area Reporter* had been torn apart page by page. Books had been ripped apart, the spines broken. The spine of *Linda Goodman's Love Signs* , over 1,100 pages of it, had been torn in shreds. I got sidetracked from calling the police, looking at the rest of Billy's books on the floor: *Body Work for Men*, Jung's *Archetypes of the Collective Unconscious, The Healing Power of Crystals, Who Dies?, Being and Doing – A Workbook for Actors*. Billy and I belonged to different cultures.

The police called me. As I bent to pick up the phone from the floor beside my chair I noticed that Billy still had the old model Phone-Mate I'd sent him seven or eight Christmases ago. I told the police to come around, then turned on the answering machine and set the dial to playback to find out anything I could about Billy's life. The tape was blank. To make certain I let it run while I looked to see if there was anything I should do before the police arrived. I'd noticed Billy's checkbook under a pile of books on the floor and I picked it up and set the tape to rewind. The checking record showed a balance of $97.03. I started trying to decipher his entries to see if the rent had been paid, then realized it would be faster to look for a large regular amount. I jumped at the sound of reversed noise on the tape: it hadn't been fully rewound when I started playing it. I tried to work out what that meant but I had trouble thinking clearly. Billy's machine had been turned off without messages being replayed, or there was something on the tape that Billy wanted to save. Had he left the house for the last time without turning on his machine?

The reverse noise lasted half a minute. I set the dial to playback once again. A pause with static, then the sound of a receiver being hung up. Someone listening after Billy's message had played. To see if he was there and picked up at the last minute? Then another hang-up. And another. And another, and another. Then the blank tape. I thought that whoever searched Billy's living room maybe turned off the machine, but either hadn't been interested in replaying the messages or had panicked before he worked out how to do it. Because he surely would have wondered if there was a message about what he was looking for.

It occurred to me to play Billy's message, though I did it with a certain dread. "This is Billy's machine," Billy said. "I don't know where he is, but if you tell me your name I'll tell him you called when he shows up again." Smart ass. His voice was strong, and he'd managed to keep his self-amusement under control. Wasn't my brother a little smug, a little self- righteous under all that non-judgmental counterculture New Age shit? And more than a little angry at the people who ran the world from which he was willing to take what he needed?

The police banged on the front door 40 minutes after they called and I tore downstairs as if they might go away again. There were two detectives, men about my age who got left behind following me up the stairs. Or maybe they really believed it was important to study the walls and ceilings as they climbed so heavily. I thought they seemed pleasant and competent, but wary, or professionally noncommittal. An hour after they left I couldn't recall their voices or how they looked or distinguish between them.

I thought I could read their minds as they glanced around the two empty rooms facing north.

"It looks as if somebody just moved out," I said, acting alert and efficient now that I had people to deal with. "I'm not so sure. Billy has lived – Billy lived alone for years after the theater collective broke up. He's lived here, okay, I'm sorry, about three years. He never mentioned a roommate and I know he didn't need help with the rent because I've been paying him rent for our house in Minneapolis for the last two years. I can't believe the rent for this place cost him under $500." Neither detective felt a need to comment on what I'd said. I felt foolish in the silence that followed me into the living room.

I'd left the mess on the floor almost as I'd found it. I told the detectives about the answering machine being turned off and showed them the pile of mail I'd picked up inside the front door.

"I've been trying to work out from the dates when the thief was here," I said. "Some of the opened letters are postmarked the 26th in San Francisco, which was Thursday, so they can't have been opened before Friday, which makes sense if Billy was found on Friday night. But there are other San Francisco letters dated the 26th that haven't been opened."

"It's not uncommon for a letter mailed locally on Thursday to be delivered on Monday," one of the detectives remarked.

"If somebody went through the mail on Friday or Saturday, and more was delivered afterwards, that would explain how arbitrary the search seems," I said. "Some letters have been opened and some haven't, without any apparent pattern. I found no personal letters. Just utility bills and a lot of mailings from AIDS organizations and junk mail. But even some of the junk mail was opened."

"Could your brother have opened the mail on his way out on Friday?"

"It was scattered all over the hall downstairs. Just dumped on the carpet. Billy wouldn't have made that kind of mess for himself. Also I can't find an address book. Also the bedroom and the kitchen don't seem to have been touched. And there are boxes of books and magazines in the smaller front room that haven't been touched. Maybe whoever was here found what he wanted. Maybe he was scared away." I ran out of steam. "Do you want some coffee?" They declined, and I went into the kitchen to be by myself for five minutes. I wondered where the cat had gone.

When I returned they were adding papers to a neat pile they'd built on the floor.

"For fingerprints," one of them said.

"Did you take anything from his wallet at the hospital?" I asked.

"There was nothing to take."

I sat on the sofa and swung my feet up beside me to be out of the way. I saw that the cat had climbed onto the back of a bookcase shelf near the window and was toasting in a puddle of sunlight between the books and the wall.

"My brother was gay, of course," I said, deciding to deal with their prejudices right away. "Also, he may have made some money from selling small amounts of recreational drugs."

One of the detectives paused and raised his head slightly in my direction, but changed his mind and went on poking through the ashes in the fireplace with the end of a pen.

"When did you arrive in San Francisco?" he asked.

"Last night," I said.

"You were in Minneapolis on Friday night and until last night?"

"Yes," I said. "Until I got Billy's message."

"Will your family be able to verify that?"

"Billy was the only family I had left," I said, as if it was the most ordinary answer in the world. I'd gotten over squirming when people asked family questions. "Maybe I saw somebody over the weekend or talked to somebody on the phone. I'll think about it."

"This looks like the remains of a supermarket log," he said. "I don't think anything else was burned here."

"How else did your brother make a living?" the other one asked.

"This and that. He worked in a bookstore for a while, and a bar that I believe went out of business. He once worked in a plant store, but I don't know which one. Billy could live on nearly nothing."

I was starting to feel disoriented. It didn't help that the police didn't look at me when they asked questions and never reacted to my answers. I was reminded of the TV nighttime soap operas where characters converse with their backs turned, facing the camera instead of each other. The police seemed less interested in what I said than in turning over the room like professional scavengers. But I wasn't taken in for a minute.

"Were you close to your brother?" He muttered it like an afterthought.

I swallowed. "I loved Billy very much," I said carefully, "and he loved me. But we didn't see very much of each other. We talked on the phone about once a month. Well, less than that the last year or so. The last time I actually saw Billy was for dinner one night at my hotel about four years ago." I remembered how I'd gone out of my way to be broadminded about his clothes when we went into the dining room. "I was here on an overnight business trip. I sort of squeezed him in." My voice broke suddenly, and I had to fight to swallow regret.

"Are you gay?"

"No," I snapped, flooding with anger and fighting for control. They were gracious enough to ignore me while I got myself together.

"I've been thinking," I said eventually.

"Yes," a detective said.

"If Billy was thrown from a car travelling at high speed, there must have been at least one other occupant apart from the driver."

"That would make sense."

"Do you have any idea what's going on?"

"It's too soon to say."

"What can I do to help?" I asked. The phone rang before I got an answer. Both detectives' heads jerked in my direction at last.

"Were you expecting a call?"

I shook my head. They nodded to me to pick it up and I moved toward the phone.

It was a woman who identified herself as belonging to Channel 7 News. "We're very sorry to hear about your brother," she lied, sounding over-friendly and tense. "We wondered if you'd be willing to speak to one of our reporters?"

After I worked out that they meant for me to be interviewed on camera, I said I'd talk if they let me appeal for help in finding Billy's killers.

"You know it's possible your brother jumped from the car," a detective said after I hung up. "In which case the question is why – was he trying to escape, or was he too intoxicated to know what he was doing? Did you know your brother was an alcoholic and a narcotics addict?"

I resisted the description. "He was always trying to stop," I said.

"We found no marks that told us anything useful about the car he fell from. If he was thrown, the question is still why."

"I know it wasn't for anything Billy did," I said. "Billy didn't hurt people and he wasn't involved with big-time dealers. When I mentioned selling drugs, I meant a small bag of grass or a few tablets of Percodan among friends."

When they finished sifting through the mess on the floor the detectives went into the bedroom to look at Billy's clothes. The only things I'd noticed in the closet this morning were a few pairs of jeans and a lot of T-shirts and one very old brown leather jacket which I was determined to keep and wear for many years to come. I also thought I could wear it in this city and not stick out like a sore thumb.

As I waited for the cops to return to the living room I felt a core of misery rising inside me. Part of it was resentment against being forced to feel so much. I hoped I wouldn't have to give in to it, not until I had nothing else to do or at least until I was alone. But memories were bombarding me, and they felt more authentic than anything happening in the apartment. I was ashamed of most of the memories, because they were sad and self-pitying: about pressing our noses against the windows of other families' houses, about needs not met so that we pretended we didn't have them, about making do with cheap thrills. Billy had left me just as the block of ice around my past was melting. I'd never be able to share memories with him or reinvent the past to suit both of us now. I was beginning to be very angry at him.

"I'd advise you to have the locks –"

"Today," I said. "Can you give me the landlord's phone number? I have his name from the cancelled checks, but I don't have his number."

"He is listed," a detective said. "How long are you planning to stay in San Francisco?"

"Until I find out what happened to Billy," I said.

"Do you have a photograph of your brother?" a detective asked.

I thought about it and shook my head. "I don't see any photographs around here. There are none in Minneapolis, except maybe old school photographs. We weren't the sort of family to take pictures." They'd finally connected with my shame.

They asked me if they could show an autopsy photograph to people they questioned and I started to cry.

The detectives said they'd stay in touch, and told me to call them with any information I thought might help, or if I found an address book. Later they called with the autopsy results – death due to the results of trauma and contributory intoxication – and then they called again twice to read me lists of names of men I'd never heard of. But until the night they took me to the police station to try to find out if I had any part in what happened, I didn't see the detectives again.

Chapter Four

"HI, I'M LUKE Carroll from Channel 7," a tall man with black curly hair announced when I opened the door, his voice rather deliberately deep and throbbing and loud enough for the street to hear. The man behind him was black and carried a video camera on his shoulder and a large bag in the other hand. Luke never bothered to introduce him, or explain why the TV crew arrived at eight o'clock, three hours later than the coordinator said they would.

After we settled facing each other for the interview, me on the couch and Luke sitting on a chair two feet away, the cameraman fiddled for a long time trying to light us. I started to apologize for the lighting. Billy's living room had only two lamps, one on the table and one at waist level next to the couch. "I'm not used to doing this myself," the cameraman said. "We've had staff cuts."

While the cameraman tried lighting experiments that didn't seem to work, Luke asked me questions in no particular order, making notes on a small pad. When had I last seen Billy? Had the police told me about possible leads? Did I have any theories about who might have wanted Billy dead? He even asked me how it felt to be in one of the AIDS capitals of America. Each time Luke mentioned Billy's death he looked appropriately grim, then he flashed his teeth encouragingly for my answer, held the ingratiating expression for a count of three, and changed it to an intelligently alert look as he listened (though once or twice I caught his eyes straying but snapping back as I seemed close to finishing). Then he looked grim and concerned again as he began the next question. Suddenly we were ready to begin taping.

"I believe you want to make an appeal to the people of San Francisco," Luke said urgently, as if he was trying to avert a disaster or at the very least was severely pressed for time.

"Yes," I said, feeling awkward. "If anyone can help me find out why Billy died, please get in touch."

"Were you aware of your brother's sexual preference?" he asked – a question he'd not asked previously.

"I knew my brother was gay," I said, trying not to look surprised or embarrassed. "Billy and I never had any secrets about his sexual preference. He was very proud of it, and I was very proud of him."

"Did you know that your brother abused alcohol and drugs?" Luke asked – another new question.

I tried to answer evenly. "Yes, but Billy was trying to stop using drugs. I know he wasn't involved in any heavy drug deals. Billy was a loving and gentle man who did not hurt other people."

The rest of Luke's questions were perfunctory. I think he had no idea what shape the broadcast interview would take and he was trying to cover all the angles.

"Do you cover crime news or gay news?" I asked Luke when the cameraman turned off his lights.

"Gay news," Luke said. "These days that's 20% crime news, because violence against gays has increased dramatically during the AIDS epidemic. Ten percent is political news, and all the rest is about AIDS, including 90% of the political news." Then he answered my unspoken question. "I'm the only openly gay reporter for a network affiliate in San Francisco. I have no secrets, so nobody can ever blackmail me." He flashed his teeth, and paused for a count of three.

I watched the eleven o'clock news on Billy's 12 inch black and white TV set, which was perched on top of a set of plastic containers for socks and underwear in the bedroom. We were the second story.

"A San Francisco man may be another victim of increased violence against gays," the co-anchor announced. "Police say he was thrown from a car on the freeway South of Market last Friday night. Channel 7 reporter Luke Carroll has the story."

"A Minneapolis attorney is in San Francisco tonight wondering why his gay older brother had to die," Luke announced, releasing the words in tense chunks while he stared into the camera as if mesmerized by his reflection.

Cut to me. "I knew my brother was gay." Cut. "Billy was trying to stop using drugs." Cut. "Billy was a gentle and loving man who did not hurt other people." The segment was almost over before I recognized the man whose voice was more familiar to me than his face: my hair was gray, and my words had the authority of middle age. When I'd talked to Luke I'd felt younger and more tentative, as if I had to fight to be believed. I protested to myself that the TV camera distorted me; at the same time I felt enhanced by the image on the screen. I thought I was foolish, like Luke, for feeling that.

"Like so many gay men, Billy Phillips came to San Francisco in pursuit of a dream of freedom to be himself," Luke concluded. "Tonight his brother is wondering who destroyed that dream."

"Police are treating the death as a homicide," the co-anchor announced. "Billy Phillips' brother has appealed for help in finding out how he died. If you can help, call this number."

That night the cat jumped up on an extreme corner of the bed when I lay down to try to go to sleep. Every time I checked he was sitting watching me with his feet curled under him. Somehow I knew he'd run away if I tried to get him to come closer.

Chapter Five

WHEN I WAS seven years old and Billy was 10 he came close to plunging a pair of garden shears into our father's chest. I remember that he did it for me. "If you ever touch me again I'll shove these in your heart," Billy sobbed, terrified at what he was doing but jabbing towards our father with the shears that were so heavy they pulled his arms down. Our mother danced back and forth in front of her husband to protect him. "But if you ever touch my brother –" Billy stopped, stymied, because he could think of nothing worse to do to our father.

"Crazy kid," our father said, his eyebrows arched high in innocence and his shiny ears, lean as cooked bacon rind, sticking out from his head. But he was only searching for what might sound like the authentic response of an innocent man. "Crazy kid," appealing to his wife, "how can a son say things like that to his father?"

"If you ever touch me again," Billy sobbed, and then he started to choke on the emotion pouring out of his body.

Our silly mother looked at both of us with disgust. For ever afterwards we managed her or used her, but we did not take her seriously.

Billy carried the key to our bedroom during the day so that nobody could steal it. One night our father tried to break down the door while our mother finally shouted no and Billy screamed for help through the window.

The caseworkers asked me if I'd been abused like my brother, and I said no, although afterwards I began to be troubled by the memory of an important visit to a dark room in a high-walled street that everyone said could only have been a dream. I don't know. I remember more of my life every day, but the revelations are involuntary: I'll never be a therapy junkie, wasting my life peeling the layers from the past until I reach levels I may be inventing instead of remembering.

I believe an arrangement was made: our mother could keep us and our father would not be prosecuted if he stayed away and sent money every month. I'm only guessing, because the caseworkers expected our mother to explain to us what had been arranged, and she was infuriatingly incapable of meeting a child's expectations. I remember once when I was even younger trying to force her to show me how to spell "mosquito." I kept writing out different attempts for her, including the one I was sure was right, and she kept smiling and saying No, that's wrong. It was years before it occurred to me that she may have been ashamed to admit she couldn't spell the word herself.

When I was ten another kid said, "Your mother is an invalid, isn't she?" Even as I flushed and vehemently denied it I realized that it was true. She'd become a recluse, which in one way made things easier for me. I'd have been ashamed to be seen with her in public as her weight ballooned. She ate; our father was drinking, wherever he was. Billy and I raised ourselves.

Billy wasn't always there. Maybe he started to feel the implications of what had happened to him once we were physically safe from our father. By the time Billy was 20 he'd been in mental hospitals for a total of three years, the last time in the state hospital where psychiatrists and nurses did to him the things it was customary to do to patients then, which still cause me to loathe every shrink I trip over. I went to see Billy in hospital (those jerry-built fortresses with their sadistic walls) every time I could get the money, to talk about when he was coming home. At last, taking longer to come home than years took to end, he'd appear smiling and I was happy again because we could begin again. We never talked about what had happened to him.

It's hard for me to imagine that Billy ever had a critical thought about me when we were kids. He never made fun of me for being bookish and precocious and ambitious. I studied psychology at the U for obvious reasons – although the connection between my life and the behavioral psychology they taught at the University of Minnesota seemed more tenuous the more courses I took – and because I'd read in an Ivy League law school bulletin at the library that "diverse undergraduate backgrounds are encouraged," which meant I didn't have to major in history or poli sci. Billy left home as soon as I started my freshman year. I wanted him to go: I was always afraid the shrinks would come to get him again. And I wanted to build a career on my own. At some point it became part of my ambition to surpass Billy – maybe because he was one of the few people who'd seen me when I was weak – until he became the dependent brother. That was easy to do.

By the time I entered Columbia Law School in 1962 Billy had been living in New York for two years. There was never a chance that I'd live with him. I went to law school to make the top ten percent in my class; Billy lived from hand to mouth in a room in the East Village, though probably more friends came to that room in a week than saw my room in a year. He'd always had more friends than I did, and more women than men, though even when I was very young I knew that his male friends were gay and that he probably had sex with most of them. At some point I made an effort to indicate to him with wordless blurred goodwill that it was okay with me, but we didn't start talking about it until the early 70's when he called and told me he was marching in the gay parade and asked me to come. I went once to watch, and became very uptight because a drunken Billy and one of his friends went up to a red-faced middle-aged cop and pretended in front of the crowd that they'd all made it together the previous night. The cop did not like the game at all. Another time I marched – by myself, because I couldn't find him in the crowd where we'd arranged to meet. I felt as if I should be carrying a printed sign explaining my status. When he called the following year and asked me to march again I said I'd probably have to work.

My loyalty and Billy's determined cool (when he was sober and not high) usually stopped me thinking too deeply about his sexuality. But I remember that once, drinking myself now, but alone, the booze encouraged a rare insight about him. It would have been hard enough for Billy to accept himself just having to fight the shrinks and the viciously ignorant religious who made a living attacking his sexuality. He also had to deal with the ultimate assault on his integrity: he'd been screwed by our father. I could see the shrinks' eyes lighting up when they heard that. No wonder he chose to live what looked to me like an unexamined life.

Not that all my education automatically led to an examined life. School was the most comfortable place in the world for me; I worked hard at the limited exercises that pass for thinking in college and in law school, and nearly always got rewarded proportionately. The professors who graded me didn't guess and probably didn't care that school was all I had. Sometimes I still catch myself expecting my daily life to be as easy. At the end of the second year at Columbia I got the anticipated offers from the giant Wall Street law firms, but chose a relatively small firm in which the father of one of my classmates was a founding partner. My classmate and I both made partner in four years. During that time I was married for two years, until my wife and I realized that I would do anything to avoid letting her know who I was. I met two or three women after her who seemed ideal to me; I never understood why we cooled towards each other so quickly, or which of us cooled first. I learned the convenience of buying whores who mimicked the looks and attitudes of the richest women I met in my law practice. Some of them protested the way I abused them. I was amused at their presumption.

I was a natural at the tunnel vision that helped me work the long hours in corporate law, focusing on the innumerable arcane details of multimillion dollar paper deals. I still don't put down the satisfaction of closing a deal, mediating a dispute, earning the respect of the other side. But I had almost nothing else in my life. Billy and I began drinking heavily in high school, and for 30 years I worked, exercised – nothing is better for easing the worst effects of a hangover – and drank. Once or twice a week I drank with my former classmate and his father, who were also drunks. Sometimes I'd have one drink with a client, no more, because it paid to feed the image of an expensive, reserved attorney from the best schools. (Early on I'd let one or two clients get to know me better, and I soon felt their puzzlement and mistrust.) But my serious drinking I did alone, on weekends and for a hard core three or four hours late every evening until I passed out.

One night during a drinking blackout I fell against a sharp-edged table in my condo. When I came to hours later my left arm was paralyzed, the nerves almost severed. I remember my irritation when a doctor kept asking me more and more questions about exactly how it had happened. I told him the phone had rung in the middle of the night and I'd stumbled over the table on my way to get it. He pointed out that the blow to my arm wasn't enough to knock me unconscious until the morning. My first night in the hospital I called outside to have a bottle delivered and it got intercepted. The doctors recommended a treatment center. I figured I needed a rest, and the arm injury explained my absence from the office. I chose Hazelden, because my insurance paid for the best, because it removed me from the possible shame of meeting someone I knew in New York, because it seemed appropriate to be going home to get well. Except that I didn't tell my mother or anyone else (there was no one else) I was back in Minnesota.

"Unwilling to explore fully the implications of his disease," someone commented about me at Hazelden. Which meant I was willing to admit I was a drunk, but unwilling to share many details of what it had done to my life, or what kind of life I'd had that fit so well with becoming a drunk. I stayed in Hazelden for three weeks, then flew back to New York and returned to work the next morning. Almost immediately, I watched my world unravel.

I knew how to stonewall, how to shut out everything but the task at hand. But without booze I couldn't stop myself feeling as raw and threatened and vulnerable as the night our father tried to break down the bedroom door in that terrible rage. I finally felt how precariously high I'd soared on the skimpiest of wings. My tunnel vision wasn't enough to keep me aloft this time. One day, out of the blue to me, my partners called me to a meeting and told me they were buying my interest in the firm. They cited irreconcilable differences in our approach to law and mentioned vague complaints from clients about my seeming unapproachable. Their initial offer was about one-quarter of what my share of the partnership was worth, although they were gracious enough to suggest I hire an attorney to negotiate the details of the settlement agreement. I was so shattered that at first I believed their reasons for getting rid of me must be true. I tried to apologize and negotiate. They made it clear I was out. Days later

I started asking myself why these issues had arisen now. I remembered how they'd stiffened when I began turning down chances to drink with them, how my classmate Mark had thrust a soda at me, not meeting my eyes, when he opened the booze for himself at a late meeting. This is what I believe happened: a group of alcoholics supported one another in their disease, one moved towards getting well, and the others got rid of him to maintain their house of cards.

But I wasn't certain. I'd depended on my profession for an identity. I discovered a rage inside me that sometimes made me think my brain would melt because I could do nothing to make it go away. Even in the rare times when I was thinking about something else I'd suddenly shift into awareness that I'd been eaten up again by my obsession.

Two months after I was kicked out of the firm our mother died, her body found days later when junk mail and newspapers started piling up. I called Billy before I left New York and left a message on his machine. When I got to the house in Minneapolis there was a message from him on the Phone-Mate I'd sent to both my mother and Billy for Christmas four or five years ago. He wasn't coming home for the funeral. He said he didn't "see much point."

I stayed on in Minneapolis because I was ashamed to go back to New York. I'd stayed so naive in my alcohol-protected bubble about the half-truths most people contrive to get by that I couldn't even concoct some story about the partnership breaking up and stick to it until I got another job. There were problems about selling the house because we didn't know if our father was still alive, and I used that as an excuse for staying on. Billy benefited, because I sent him half of a rather generously estimated monthly rental figure while I lived there. One muggy night, alone in the suffocating rooms where I'd grown up, my body itching with mosquito bites from that day's run along the Mississippi, in a rage I had to quench, I drank again, and from then on I was drunk all day. A month later I almost lost my life in a blackout when I drove my car off a freeway ramp.

Straight from the hospital I checked into Hazelden again. I still didn't buy everything they told me. They said alcoholics can't afford resentments, so I went through the motions of writing down all the reasons I was to blame for what my partners had done to me. But I only did it because I had to, because survival is the best revenge. I did recognize how I'd checked out of the best part of each day for nearly 30 years. I realized how little I knew about things most people value most, which I probably despised when I wasn't feeling shut out. I had one relationship, with Billy, that had endured, sort of, while we systematically wrecked our lives. When I got sober the second time that relationship didn't seem as perfect. I'd deserted Billy, I'd patronized him. It also seemed he'd succeeded in teaching me to let him off easy. He'd never let us be sounding boards for each other; there'd never been give and take or truly intimate connection. Apart from looking down on him the way I looked down on anyone who hadn't made it with their brains, I'd suspended judgment about his part-time jobs that made political or artistic statements, his activism in various causes that never earned him a cent and which I'd supported with crisis money over the years. I didn't know what I really thought about gay men. Billy was gay, so gay was automatically good, at least as long as Billy stayed gay.

I lived in the house in Minneapolis for another two years. I forced myself to go to a lot of A.A. meetings even though they bored me or made me angry. I even had a meeting at my house on Thursdays at six. Except on the days I hid at home in a funk, I ran in all kinds of weather along the river and around the lakes, and raced on weekends, taking a taxi to the starting line because my license had been revoked. If I missed even a day I felt heavy and slow and had to recreate my picture of myself as a minor athlete before I could force myself out the door again.

I loved watching and smelling the Minneapolis seasons, the long winter and summer, the flooding three-week spring and the fall that sometimes lasted seven or eight weeks if the snow didn't start in October. Sometimes I went into Dinkytown and ate alone at student restaurants to watch the kids. I felt like an adolescent starting over with none of the skills to serve my deepest needs. At the same time I noticed that I'd grown older – irritable with the young, impatient with people who were poor or slow, and fearful of the future, although I tried to hide that fear from myself – and it seemed to have happened overnight. Even senses I thought I could trust were affected. When I shaved I saw an ambitious young attorney still hoping to move the earth, not a still shaky recovering alcoholic of 47 with his life in ruins.

One day I picked up a copy of the *Daily* someone had left in a runners' store and found a tribute to a U of M psychology professor who'd killed himself at the age of 65. I'd gone to some of his classes and used him as an advisor on an undergraduate project. He'd been a maverick, living in Minneapolis without a car, espousing "unscientific" subjects like ageing and grief, proclaiming his bisexuality *and* his celibacy. I remembered how I'd patronized him. Even then I'd dismissed imagination and joy, I suppose because I wasn't certain where they'd lead me, and I didn't know how to ask anyone for help.

I called Billy after I left Hazelden the second time and told him I'd gotten sober and thought that if I drank again I'd probably die. Billy said he was pleased for me and mentioned he'd been to N.A. and A.A. meetings off and on. I wished him luck, and left it at that because I was afraid of losing him the way I'd lost my partners.

Even before I went back to Hazelden, as I lay alone and trapped in an empty hospital room that echoed my empty life, I vowed that nothing would ever be as important to me again as not drinking. I'd never be angry enough, or lonely enough, or enough in love, or have strong enough feelings about anything that I wanted to take a drink.

Then somebody killed my brother Billy.

Chapter Six

FOR TWO DAYS I waited by the phone for help that didn't come. I left the house only long enough to maintain sanity, for two long runs and to eat dinner and go to evening A.A. meetings in a church basement off Union Square. If anyone in those smoky rooms did recognize me from the TV interview, they didn't let on; recovering alcoholics are not famous for a passionate interest in keeping up with the news. I still felt raw, but distanced from what was going on around me, as if I was walking underwater. Curiously, I think I saw more of the city than if I'd felt connected. Later I'd remember those days in San Francisco the way I remembered Paris the first time I saw it, on my first vacation from the New York law firm, the first vacation of my life, when I finally had money and still believed in a future. The richness and color of both cities overwhelmed me. Cities are easier for me to get along with than individuals.

I'd known San Francisco the way I'd known every city I went to on business. I stayed in a downtown hotel, met with clients or other attorneys in the financial district, dined with them at a recommended restaurant and had tourist attractions pointed out to me in passing. I'd seen Golden Gate Park before because local counsel once drove me through it on the way to a meeting at the Cliff House.

Now I sought out the parts of the city where Billy had lived. The house he'd lived in was a faded navy blue, with bay windows facing the street on both floors. The rest of that side of the street, edging the black ghetto, was a mishmash of ugly apartment buildings, but on the north side there was a row of three- or four-story houses, each a different height with different wooden detailing and window design. Some had deteriorated, others were gentrified and brightly-painted in contrasting colors. The street felt shabby and dirty – the whole city felt dirty after Minneapolis, the way New York felt when I first moved there – because the road and sidewalks were broken and littered. But one day running home I turned the corner and was surprised by the bright pretty houses baking in the sun. Perhaps any street would feel shabby to me in my present mood. During the first ten days I lived in Billy's apartment workmen built four two-story wooden houses on a vacant corner directly opposite our empty front rooms. I stood at the window and watched when I was at a loss what to do next. Building the houses looked easier than I'd imagined, which I supposed meant they were easy to tear down. I always expected houses to last, while the people in them moved on. Tenants moved into the new houses a day or two after the workmen finished them.

The street was near Church and Market, a block from where the N Judah underground train surfaced from the downtown tunnel. I was three doors away from a park four blocks long, a green rectangle bordered with trees and bushes on a hill that climbed past a hospital to the block where Castro Street hit Divisadero. To the south on Castro, down the hill, was the gay residential and shopping district that was the mecca of the life Billy belonged to for nearly 20 years.

The heat wave continued for most of each day, broken by a couple of overcast windy days. I ran in the late afternoon to avoid the worst of the heat. Some days the weather was already turning chilly by four o'clock; on other days the air was still heat-laden on my wet skin when I reached home at six. The first day I ran I crossed Divisadero and kept climbing the residential hills to the bottom of Buena Vista Park, then turned right, downhill across Haight Street to the Panhandle, a small ruler-shaped park where groups of men, black and white and Asian, usually racially separated, played basketball and practiced martial arts. The Panhandle leads to Golden Gate Park, which is also ruler-shaped, a four mile downhill run to the ocean. The second day I ran uphill for 30 minutes to the top of Twin Peaks, with its 360 degree view of the city bleached and complacent in the sunshine. From the top of the hill San Francisco looked like a spectacular hilly island surrounded by sea and other islands and connected to some of them by bridges. Lush spring was everywhere: flowering trees and gardens and overflowing planters outside the houses; waves of red and yellow and purple wildflowers and grasses of a dozen different greens spilling down the hillsides; layers of trees I couldn't name, tall or squat and lacy or solid with leaves, receding for miles in Golden Gate Park. The city pounded for attention on the glass wall that cut me off from it.

I was no stranger to gay neighborhoods; when I lived in New York I'd eaten regularly in the Village and gone to movies at the Waverly. I'd had gay classmates and colleagues and usually made an effort to be friendly to them, maybe to find out something from them about Billy that I didn't already know, although they seemed wary of me. But the men on Castro, with whom Billy presumably shared his life, were exotic unknowns to me. At the corner of Castro and Market a bald man in his forties wearing a Golds Gym muscle shirt and a black leather jacket, a green feather earring dangling from his right ear, waited for the light with his arm around a pale, pudgy girl in a grubby T-shirt and jeans. Two men in business suits pecked each other on the lips outside the underground Muni station. Two young women with clean short hair crossed Market holding hands. They wore identical Reeboks and similar pairs of aviator glasses and they had the becalmed look of students who worked but didn't give the teacher a hard time. Thin and unhealthy young men and women, swamped in shapeless black cotton jackets and pants, with cloth slippers on their feet, pretended to be unaware of the effect on the rest of us of their painted faces and hair. But I thought I recognized what was behind their attempt to deaden their eyes: fear of a world still largely unknown to them. I thought that to provoke its resentment was a promising start. Men of all ages lumbered behind huge pectorals that preceded the rest of their bodies. I'd lived my life with men whose bodies were shaped by function. Those of us who were fit had bodies toned by exercise, but until I went to the Castro I thought serious bodybuilding was only for certain athletes who required the strength and for blue collar workers who needed an inexpensive interest outside their dead-end jobs. The men I saw on the Castro were all shapes and ages and colors – although most of the blacks, men and women, seemed to be there to beg – but with shorter hair, more beards, a lot more moustaches, and tighter and more colorful clothes than I was used to seeing in straight districts of Minneapolis or New York. I found that the district had some of the advantages of a neighborhood. The clothes in the Castro stores were less expensive than the classic clothes I was used to wearing, and the food in the coffee shops cost half what I paid when I ate downtown.

On the corner of Castro and 18th Street I nearly tripped over a toddler. His mother, who might have been one of my former law associates, retrieved her child while her husband went on explaining the culture to an older man and woman who looked slightly dazed around the eyes: "Gay men in San Francisco changed their sexual behavior when AIDS surfaced," the young husband said, as if he'd been hired to do a promotion.

Across the street in Walgreens I waited in line behind a young man in his mid-20's. He was no slimmer than a lot of the men his age on the street, but his facial skin was red and dry. He seemed to know the clerk, and pointed to the deodorant stick he was buying and the brown envelope under his arm. "They're sending me into the hospital overnight for tests," he said. "Good luck," the clerk said with a brief smile that was almost a shrug. They both had a business-as-usual attitude that I recognized from my own reaction when I regained consciousness after the accident. I didn't waste much time regretting my broken body. For all I know, the aftershocks continue for ever, unbalancing us when we least expect them, but for most of us the immediate reaction to disaster is to accept it as overdue, something we thought we'd be forced to get acquainted with, and then we see how we can survive with what's left.

On Castro I saw young men whose faces had been dusted with ash, who swivelled their bodies behind walking sticks and inched across intersections long after the light had turned against them, skin emptying sweat into clothes (though I'd have thought those fragile bird bodies didn't have any surplus liquid) as the line of drivers up the hill honked at the unseen obstruction. I saw two tall men together, skin hanging so cleanly on their bodies that the bone shone through, their eyes bright in darkened sockets. They were helping each other shop, enjoying the window displays and the last of the sun.

My fourth morning in the city I ran ten miles to the ocean and back at eight o'clock, when the sky was already blue and the sun yellow but not yet burning. When I got back to the house two young girls were sitting on the steps. I think they were 10 or 11, but I'd been away from children so long I couldn't be sure. One of them started to giggle when she saw my running shorts soaked with sweat. I stood outside my door digging for my keys in the pocket inside the shorts while I tried not to pull the waistband too far away from my body. The girl leaned back on the step and looked up, her face under my crotch, and opened her mouth and stuck out her tongue and lapped in my direction while her friend shrieked.

After I showered I called Channel 7 and left a message for Luke Carroll. He called me three hours later.

"I need a friend," I said. "If you help me find out what happened to Billy you can have the story."

Pause. "I'll call you tonight when I'm through," Luke said.

Chapter Seven

LUKE LIVED IN the hills northwest of the Castro, in a garden apartment in a brown stucco building that even on the outside was a remarkably shabby home for a TV newsman. As soon as he opened the door I saw that he was upset. At the same time, next to the hall door, I noticed a poster for a production of the men's theater collective Billy had belonged to.

"Maybe some of those men know what Billy was up to recently," I said.

Luke almost glared at me, as if I was foolish or redundant. He bumped into me as he closed the door behind me. I smelled alcohol on his breath at the same time that I was trying not to let my body pull back from him. I needed him to think I trusted him.

The living room was large, with sliding glass doors opened onto a small tree-enclosed space with bushes and flowers, but the furniture inside was mostly of the wooden garden variety. The sofa which was the only thing left free to sit on was covered with an itchy tartan cloth. There were a few square feet of worn brown carpet left clear in front of the sofa. The rest of the floor was hidden under what looked like the contents of a high tech showroom that hadn't been organized: a projection TV four feet across, a smaller monitor and two VCR's with stacks of cassettes piled precariously on chairs and against the walls, laser and compact disc players, a PC with a laser printer, two hooked up stereos and enough separate components to make up one or two more systems. Some of the electronic parts still sat on the boxes they'd been shipped in even though they were plugged in; other boxes hadn't been unpacked. I saw what looked like a Nautilus system through the open bedroom door. To move around the living room was to navigate through equipment. There was nothing else in the room except posters on the walls celebrating mostly gay events and causes.

Luke paused in the archway to the kitchen, where he kept the booze. "I covered a memorial service for the founder of the collective three months ago," he said. "Three more of the original members already died of AIDS. One got married and is raising kids in Oregon. One moved back to Boston years ago. One lives in L.A. and produces straight porno tapes. Although that may be a dying art, if you see what I mean." He showed me his teeth and splashed wine into a tumbler as if he'd been waiting impatiently to use me as a reason for another drink. I shook my head when he held out the glass. He came and sat beside me and immediately pulled a bag from beneath a cushion and began to roll a joint. I recognized in him the comforting anticipation that I'd watched in Billy when he began the smoking ritual. Behind us through the open doors the garden swam in heat and darkness.

"I did a six o'clock report on community relations between gay men and lesbians," Luke said. "Two lesbians have already called the news director to complain that a report by a gay man is bound to be inherently biased. They're even saying my job ought to be shared by a gay man and woman."

I declined the joint, trying to be casual and neutral, hoping that Luke wouldn't get stoned.

"Which is total bullshit," Luke said, smoking with rather spacious gestures, as if he was trying to control shaking. "I've been working in the industry since college and I've been out of the closet since college and got turned down for countless jobs because of it. I just kept reapplying on the basis of my credentials until I became a fact that wouldn't go away, till I made myself interesting. Now some dyke thinks she deserves equal time in the limelight because if a gay man gets it because he worked for it she ought to get it for nothing."

"I'm sure that's not likely to happen," I said, trying to sound as if I really cared.

"No it isn't," Luke said, talking to the smaller TV screen. "But

I'm angry at even the suggestion. If dykes want equal time, let them suffer through AIDS. Dykes have to be one of the three most underemployed minorities in this town. They've existed on part-time jobs and what they call networking with their friends, which never leads to anything except another low-paying part-time job. AIDS has been a godsend to dykes. They're the population that's the least at risk from AIDS in America, yet they have half the AIDS jobs in the city, because you don't actually need any qualifications for most of the jobs and because it was politically correct to hire women and because the gay men who head up the organizations felt less threatened professionally by women than by other men. Although now I think they're realizing they should have felt threatened. As soon as the dykes got the jobs they started using the time that was funded to take care of gay men to start discussing their trivial bullshit issues: "Lesbians and AIDS," "The problems of lesbians working with gay men." I once covered a seminar where a dyke social worker spent 30 minutes complaining how badly she felt when she visited an AIDS patient to talk about benefits and he had a stereo she couldn't possibly afford on her salary. Which was four times what she'd earned before AIDS came along. Dykes and gay men have *absolutely* nothing in common. I have far more in common with straight men and women. At least we all like men."

Luke dragged away at the joint as if it were a cigarette and got up and poured himself more wine. "You know the worst thing about dykes?" I shook my head, still trying to look interested. "They're the most excruciatingly boring human beings on earth. They're either consumed with sexual heat and can't stop talking about trying to bang every woman they meet, or they're in emotional heat, just longing for a cozy merger, and they can't stop talking about that, which is even more boring. Either way they're bone-crushingly humorless and totally oblivious to anything except their own so-called issues."

He finished the joint and turned and faced me. He was more muscular and even taller than me; I felt it even when we were sitting down, and it caused me problems.

"Sorry," he said, and grinned, a little shamefaced about revealing his concerns. "Nobody is going to steal my job. Or my dope. There used to be good sex as well. The more the merrier." He whooped, watching to see how I reacted. I think he knew he had a captive audience and wanted to watch me squirm a little. "But that isn't in the cards these days, not the sleazy go-for-broke kind I used to like. Did Billy tell you what it used to be like?"

"Not a lot," I said, but Luke hadn't waited for an answer.

"Some day when I have nothing to lose I'll devote a chapter of my memoirs to the way it was. I used to check into a South of Market bathhouse at eight o'clock on Friday night and emerge for an early dinner and some sleep late on Sunday afternoon. I consumed quite a lot of drugs during those weekends and got on intimate terms with quite a lot of men. Most of whom I don't remember." He grinned again, then I'm sure quite deliberately made his face go sad, still watching for my reactions. "And many of whom are dead or dying. I remember thinking as I looked at those bathhouse carpets a few inches from my face and stiff with all kinds of bodily fluids that the bathhouses were just a breeding ground for some disaster."

"Those days will come again if you really want them to," I said, to establish how nonjudgmental I was.

"No!" Luke scoffed.

"Yes they will," I said. "There's nothing new under the sun. They'll find a way of controlling AIDS like any other disease and one day the party will start all over again."

"I'll be too old to enjoy the next time," Luke said.

I laughed, because he must have been 15 years younger than me. "Give it ten years," I said. "Did you know my brother?"

"Not that I know of," Luke said. "But I could have. Everybody in San Francisco has met everybody else, although they might not be in a condition to remember it."

"I'm sure he was very much a part of the bar scene, and I'm sure he went to bathhouses."

"Then I surely met him," Luke said.

Then I said something spontaneously, because I wanted to believe it. "Billy was trying to give up drinking and drugs."

Luke's response was to start fixing another joint. "Like all my friends," he said. "Half the people I used to hang out with who aren't dead are in A.A. I look at them and I see myself two or three years from now. Shades of the prison house."

"I thought gay A.A. might be a good place to look for people who knew Billy," I said. "I got a San Francisco directory, but there are a lot of gay meetings. I'm not sure where to start."

"Start with the Diamond Street meetings," Luke said. "There's a big meeting vulgarly known as the Dating Game. That was a hot meeting the last time I was there a couple of years ago." He turned away to gulp his wine and concentrate on his joint.

I considered the implications. At first I thought he meant he'd been to a meeting to do a story, but A.A. meetings are closed to the media. While I hesitated Luke turned to me again. "I was in the program for a while," he said. "Once I got the job at Channel 7 I didn't need it any more. The work is too important for me to let myself ever get seriously screwed up again."

"I'm in the program," I said.

"I guessed," he said carelessly. "Who else would turn down a smoke and a drink in this city?"

"You're all I've got," I said to his profile. As soon as I said it I knew there was a sexual tease included in the statement. Which was fine with me. Anything to get him on my side. I was sure Luke had his pick of sex partners. All I had going for me was that I was straight, but I figured it was worth something. "I don't care how much you drink. Drinkers are a lot more interesting than recovering alcoholics. Being with you is kind of like watching the TV special versus having to wade through the book."

Luke laughed as if I'd forced him to. "Do you mind if we watch my report?" he asked, already staring at the screen and firing with the remote. It wasn't quite eleven o'clock, so he kept the sound down even though he seemed to prefer watching the screen to turning his head to me.

"There's something that bothers me," I said. "Even after the interview with you not a single friend of Billy's called me to say they're sorry he's dead. The number's listed. There hasn't been a single letter. I'd thought of having some kind of memorial service, but I know no one to invite and I can't find his address book. What's going on? Isn't this supposed to be a very tightly-knit caring community?"

"They usually announce memorial services in the B.A.R.," Luke said, still staring at the silent garbage on TV. "You can rely on a few people showing up no matter who dies. I always say it's fortunate they print names and photographs in the B.A.R. obituaries. Otherwise we wouldn't recognize our friends in the saints they write about."

I laughed, and Luke turned to face me. I was glad he looked friendly. "Maybe Billy's friends are waiting for you to get in touch with them," he said.

"We think the address book may have been stolen," I said.

"We've institutionalized death from AIDS, not from accident or murder," Luke said. "Everyone is tired. Billy's death is one death after thousands. By now we all have a whole crowd of friends and lovers dead or dying of AIDS. The men who've worked with AIDS since the beginning, since '82 or '83, are dead or dying themselves or burned out with not much left to give. The survivors are hardened. They want to survive above all else. Maybe some people know or suspect how Billy died and they're afraid to get involved. Or maybe they don't care."

Luke paid the rest of his joint more attention than the lead stories on the eleven o'clock news. I tried watching to escape depression, but the news matched my mood. It was a time of corruption, with new lies revealed each day. I noticed that no one was corrupt enough to lack supporters who defended or excused his actions.

"A report earlier tonight by Channel 7's Luke Carroll has already caused controversy," one of the anchors announced. "Members of San Francisco's lesbian community have called us charging that a report by a gay man on relations between the city's gay men and women is bound to be quote inherently biased unquote. We're repeating Luke's report in its entirety to give viewers another chance to judge for themselves."

Cut to an earnest Luke – teeth and eyes bright and glistening, skin looking impermeable, as if it had been layered with shellac – waiting with a microphone in a corridor at City Hall. "It's over four years since Supervisor Harry Britt set aside dreams of becoming San Francisco's first openly gay congressman," Luke announced. He paused, gazing into the camera to establish credibility. I glanced at Luke beside me. He was watching himself open-mouthed, even his drink and joint forgotten. He was entranced.

"Many San Francisco gay men blamed Britt's 4,000 vote defeat on the front page endorsement of eventual winner Nancy Pelosi by the editor of a feminist newspaper. That editor is a lesbian. In the closed hothouse system that is gay politics in San Francisco these things are not forgotten. The lesbian community charges that since Britt's defeat no lesbian has been elected to major public office through the votes of gay men."

Cut to young gay male activist: "Of course people don't forget. There's no doubt that the endorsement created a division within the community when it should have been concentrating on getting Harry elected."

Cut to young lesbian activist: "If anything the lesbian endorsement of Nancy Pelosi helped Harry Britt, because it rallied gay men who otherwise might not have bothered to vote for him."

Cut to Luke: "Whatever part that endorsement played in Britt's defeat, and we should point out that many lesbians voted for Britt and worked for his campaign, and that Britt went on to become President of the Board of Supervisors, the resulting bitterness focused attention on differences between the city's gay and lesbian communities, differences which some insiders say have always been far deeper than members of the straight community realize. What has happened to those differences?"

Cut to older lesbian activist: "It's true that we've always had different bars, different restaurants, different bookstores."

Cut to older gay male activist: "I think lesbians have envied the greater visibility of gay men. The women have tended to be more private. We've even cornered the market on a highly-publicized terminal illness, although I think lesbians would have to be extremely sick to envy that."

Cut to a horde of women in black leather riding motorbikes up Market Street.

Cut to Luke: "Lesbians aren't always invisible, particularly as they head the city's annual gay parade." He paused, showed his teeth, then continued: "Gay and lesbian leaders point to women's involvement in the AIDS crisis as one way gay men and women have moved closer together."

Cut to male director of organization offering support and information to AIDS patients: "Over half our staff members are women, and a third of our volunteers are women. Most of those women are lesbians. We couldn't offer the services we offer without lesbians."

Cut to Luke: "And individual gay men and women are forging bonds which are bound to lead to closer ties within the community."

43

Cut to middle-aged gay man: "The mother of my son and daughter is a lesbian. She has her female lover and I have my male lover. We all take turns raising the children."

Cut to Luke, smiling at a winning conclusion: "I'm Luke Carroll for Channel 7 News."

Cut to female anchor: "Thank you, Luke, for an interesting, if controversial, report." Thoughtful pause. She turned to the male anchor. "It's interesting to learn that there may be differences between members of a community that we've always thought of as very close knit."

The male anchor nodded. "And interesting to learn of the things men and women are doing to mend those differences."

"It's interesting," Luke said, "that some dykes can't relate to gay men unless they have a terminal illness." He punched off the TV. "Actually some dykes start to get bearable once they reach 50."

I thought that the information in the report could have been contained in two inches of newsprint, and been used to support almost any argument about its topic. I'd rather have watched shots of gay neighborhoods or meetings, with voice-over, than Luke's transparent strategies.

"Actually," Luke said, starting to look wilted and unfocused as soon as he disappeared from the screen, "everyone in the AIDS industry got caught in a trap. The jobs are uglier and meaner now that the IV drug users are pouring into the clinics and agencies. They're not white bread middle-class jobs any more, with decor furnished with gay money."

"Do you cover that in Part 2 tomorrow?" I asked.

"That's all there is," Luke said, surprised, and pouring more wine.

I'd learned to get away from situations where serious drinking took place. "Well," I said, "I'll let you know if I get any leads at the meeting."

"I'll drive you home," Luke said. "The black BMW outside is mine."

"No," I said hastily. "I need the air."

"You must be wondering what happened to forgiveness and harmony," Luke said at the door.

"The program says drunks can't afford resentments," I said. "What I really think is that if someone chooses to be your enemy you should take a little time and beat him down until his head is level with the ground and then drive a nail through his skull to keep him there." Luke hooted. "But the program says," I added, "that recovering drunks who think like that always end up drinking again."

In the middle of the night I woke up sweating under an unusual weight. The cat was curled against the edge of the pillow behind me, his rump pushing against the back of my neck. I guessed he'd finally conceded that he needed me, and I lay there loathe to disturb him, though he added to all the day's accumulated heat in the bedroom. I'd tried sleeping with the windows open, but insects from the back gardens started to attack me like Mississippi mosquitos. I moved cautiously to press the light button on my digital watch to see how much of the night was left, but the display was illegible. I edged out of bed to turn on the light and the cat stirred and complained. When I looked back at the bed he'd raised his head to watch me but he was still lying against the pillow. There was a stainless steel tag attached to his collar. I left the light on and moved slowly back to the bed and lay down with my head beside him. His green eyes darkened with caution, but he didn't jerk away when I reached out to touch the steel tag. His name was Tom. The other side of the tag was engraved with Billy's phone number and the apartment address. Billy wasn't careless about everything.

While I helped myself get to sleep in the usual way the cat moved in against my arm and moved with me. I'd heard that men who wanted to get a psychiatric discharge told the army shrinks they jerked off eight times a day. That meant I'd been half-mad for 40 years.

Chapter Eight

THERE WERE AT least 100 men in the low-ceilinged schoolroom, which was large enough to double as a dining room or assembly hall during the day: A.A. hired schoolrooms or church basements by the hour. The secretary of the meeting had taped some of the best-known program slogans to the wall: "Easy Does It," "First Things First," "Think Think Think." If my old law school professors had seen me in that room they'd have assumed my mind had turned to mush.

One at a time I'd have had no doubts about each man's sexual preference – I've learned there are a hundred small differences between straight and gay men, adding up to two almost separate sets of the needs that rule our lives – but I don't think I stood out in the crowd at that meeting. The men looked masculine enough, although some wore skimpier clothes than you'd see in a group of middle-class straight men. The conversations I overheard were about the usual topics: difficulties with people and work and cars. Although the crowded room was uncomfortably warm after another hot day, the air felt electric rather than lazy, I assumed with the sexual ambitions of a weekend night. But I've been in a room with a group of straight lawyers where the air felt similarly charged with professional ambition.

I'd expected a grimmer group of men. They belonged to a community where perhaps one man in ten came down with AIDS each year, and almost one in two carried the virus, like a time bomb with an uncertain, often protracted explosion date. But the room felt no gloomier than the straight A.A. meetings I'd gotten sober in. Which made sense when I thought about it. The recovering alcoholics who manage to remain sober are usually grateful to have been rescued from one deadly disease; they tend to see the worst disasters as a challenge to stay sober. I was grateful too, but I didn't like to have to go to rooms where the common language was a code of cliches.

The secretary asked if there were any newcomers present, and seven or eight men raised their hands. "I'm John and I'm an alcoholic." "Hi John!" 100 voices called. Loud applause. "I'm Ralph, I'm an alcoholic and a drug addict." More applause. "I'm Harold, and I'm not sure but I think I may have a drinking problem." Delighted laughter. "Hi Harold!" Applause. One of the newcomers looked about 16 but already he had the crusty burnt facial skin of a street drunk. The others resembled middle-managers at a conference, looking as if their main trouble was embarrassment at having to introduce themselves to so many people. Drunks are good at keeping up appearances against all odds, just as the language A.A. uses glosses lifetimes lived on the edge of ruin or death.

"Are there any visitors from outside the Bay Area who would like to introduce themselves?" the secretary asked. There were visitors from Houston and Sacramento and the Russian River. I raised my hand last; the secretary didn't see me right away and was starting to introduce the speaker. Men pointed in my direction.

"Yes," he said. "Go ahead."

"I"m an alcoholic visiting from Minneapolis," I said. "I'm also Billy Phillips' brother and I'm here to find out how my brother died."

Heads turned and necks craned. I was sitting in a short row of the non-smoking section at the side of the room and I could feel the attention of the men behind riveted on the back of my head. I did not like drawing attention to myself; I tried to search the wall of pleasant, curious faces for a telltale expression, but all I saw was a blur.

The speaker was Iris, a blonde woman in her 50's, a professionally feisty old broad with a throaty voice. Her presence explained the handful of women sitting together near the front, middle-aged or elderly and apparently straight, all come to the gay meeting to hear their friend speak.

"I used to tell my family it was better for me to stay home and drink a couple of bottles of wine," Iris said, "than go out to bars when I'd meet some man who'd persuade me to be unfaithful to my husband. My husband finally confronted me and told me I had a drinking problem. 'Your attitude to my drinking is my drinking problem,' I told him." Surges of laughter. She enjoyed reading and playing to us, pausing for the laughs that came every time she told the story.

I began to feel sad as I listened to the laughter, because it seemed to me that even other alcoholics were better at forming ties with other men and women than I was. I remembered my bewildered anger after I graduated from law school, when I resented having to waste time on getting on with the secretary the firm assigned to me, who insisted on treating me as an adversary. Iris could have been that secretary. Not drinking wasn't enough to protect you from the pain of learning to live in the world again. I still felt like a cripple in the world.

The meeting ended with everyone holding hands and saying the Lord's Prayer, which I was pleased to hear the man next to me mangle loudly: "Our Ho-hum, who art in Hayward, Hollywood be thy name."

I stood and waited, searching eager Friday night faces for an impulse to talk to me. Just as I was thinking I didn't seem to be on anyone's mind, I met the eyes of an older man I'd caught looking at me before, and he came over.

"I knew your brother Billy well," he rasped, "and I just wanted you to know that I loved him very much."

"I was beginning to think Billy had no friends," I said.

"Your brother was one of the most spiritual men I've ever met," he said, clasping my hand in his hands. "He never said much, but I could see it in his face."

"Who'd have wanted to kill Billy?"

"That I don't know," he said. I pulled my hand away. "I only knew him from meetings. I don't think he'd been to this meeting for quite a long time. But he had such a spiritual light about him. I'll always remember that."

"Thank you," I said.

I waited again in the corner of the room, surrounded by space while the men filed out or joked in groups. I'd noticed that people were more likely to talk to me if I was talking to someone else, so I joined the line to congratulate the speaker. She barely acknowledged me, not taken in by me for a moment, and while I thanked her she turned away to an enthusiastic friend.

"I'd like to have dinner with you one night."

The man grabbing my hand was very young, 24 or 25, and short, and wearing glasses. "I'm Roger," he said.

"Did you know my brother?"

"I don't think so," he said. "But I'd like to have dinner with you." He stared at me, his eyes soft.

"I'm not sure what I'm going to be doing for the next few days," I said.

"I won't jump on you," he said, I think trying to sound amused rather than rejected.

"Sorry," I said, and headed towards the door.

Another man was waiting for me outside, stocky, dark and bearded. "Call me," he said, and gave me a card he had ready in his hand. He moved off towards the parking lot before I could look at it under a street lamp: "Lev – Massage," and a telephone number.

Later I lay in bed watching a rerun of a cop show about a series of freeway murders (maybe I'd be happier if I really believed they were trying to send me a message through the TV), while my mind flooded with the wrong thoughts: Lev is another dead end, this whole search is futile, nothing I do ever comes to any good. I was used to surprising myself in such spontaneous heartsick litanies even when I wasn't grieving the death of a brother: at Hazelden the second time I'd learned I fit the general profile of the drunk as a man with a strong ego and poor self-esteem who spends most of his time feeling sorry for himself. If I waited through it something generally happened to distract me. This time I heard Tom purring or caught the movement as he rolled over on his back. He was stretched out at the bottom of the bed, four paws in the air, exposing his belly, tail flailing, throat pulled back with his head and nose buried in the sheets so that he could gaze at me upside down. I reached down to rub his belly, but he guided my fingers with his paws and pushed his body around until my hand was on the back of his neck. Somehow I knew exactly what he wanted. I grabbed a hunk of flesh behind his ears and pulled his body all the way up the bed until his head was under my armpit. His purring soared in ecstatic throaty breaks. He lay back and looked over his shoulder at me, then thrust his head against my chin, digging his nose and whiskers against the stubble. He shook himself, glancing at me appreciatively while the flesh and fur on his neck settled back against the bone, and staggered to the bottom of the bed, where he collapsed on his back, paws in the air again. We repeated the ride five or six times that night, and every night afterwards. I always grew sleepy or impatient before he did. Each time he reached my armpit he'd throw his face against my chin, maybe rooting for Billy's beard.

Chapter Nine

I CALLED LEV'S number as soon as I woke up the next morning and let it ring long after there was reasonable hope of getting an answer. I started dialling the number compulsively, trapped in helplessness: Where could I go for help amongst ordinary people who betrayed no sign of the evil or desperation that had killed Billy? I caught myself beginning to entertain innocent explanations of his death. Then guilt spurred me into action almost before I knew what I was doing. Billy had told me he was doing volunteer work with AIDS patients, so I spent the morning going through his back copies of local gay newspapers making a list of organizations where he might have worked.

I finally reached Lev just before noon.

"Oh yes," he said. "Give me a minute to put it together."

I repeated my statement of purpose for my benefit as well as his. "I'm trying to find out what really happened to my brother Billy."

From his hesitation I thought he might be deciding just how much to say next. "There's somebody I think you should talk to," Lev said. "I know I have his number because I just talked to him." It took him a long time to find the number; I thought he wasn't sure whether to give it to me.

"What's his name?"

"What?"

"What's the name of the person I'm supposed to talk to at this number?"

"Oh." Laughter. "Jerry. With a J."

"Okay. When can I talk to you?"

"What about?"

"You said you could help me."

"I think you should talk to Jerry. I think he's the one who can help you."

"All right, Lev. Maybe I'll see you at a meeting."

"Sure thing. Although I don't go to many meetings these days. Good luck."

When I dialled Jerry's number I got a recording with a message in a teasing, smarmy voice: "If you don't leave a message you'll never know what I could do for you."

I left my name and number and said Lev had told me to call.

I went out running at lunchtime to clear my head. As I was triple-locking the front door behind me the door of the next apartment opened. My neighbor was a handsome middle-aged woman with great presence. She was in a hurry but she softened when she saw me.

"I'm Billy Phillips' brother," I said.

"I saw you on television," she said. "I was very sorry to hear about your brother. He was never any trouble as a neighbor." She went no further in introducing herself.

"Did you ever see him with anybody? Is there anything that would help me find out what happened?"

"The police already questioned my family," she said. "He was never inside our house. He was by himself every time I saw him."

I searched her face for a sign of deceit and couldn't find it.

As I ran up to Divisadero the park on my right was scattered with sunbathers, all men, in brightly colored briefs. One man lay on his stomach and toasted a pale naked butt in the sun. The city was flowering profusely in the heat.

Back at the house a girl of 14 or 15 was standing outside the open door of the next apartment, shouting at a baby screaming in her arms. "You shut your fucking mouth, you hear, or I'm gonna beat your fucking ass!"

I cringed for the uninterrupted generations of abused children. When she didn't bother to move for me I squeezed past her and thankfully closed the door behind me.

"SHUT YOUR FUCKING MOUTH!"

I called AIDS clinics and projects, committees, foundations, groups, and asked if Billy had worked for them. Whoever answered the phone always referred me to someone else who generally wondered why the call had been referred to them. I ended up leaving my name and number 18 or 19 times. The public relations director of one organization called back, days later, to say she had no record of Billy volunteering for them. I never heard from the others.

The managing partner of my law firm clung by his fingertips to the edge of the elevator shaft, a space age tunnel which converged to a black point far below him. I wanted to bask in his terror and then his agony – I wanted to break his body beyond repair – but as his eyes protruded at me I still hesitated to push him. Half the fun of revenge is hot suffering for it. I wondered how far the police would pursue the matter if there were no witnesses. As a corporate attorney I knew next to nothing about criminal law or forensic science. Suppose he clutched at me as he fell? Mightn't they find microscopic cell clusters from my skin under his fingernails to use as evidence?

My attention shifted to Luke on the TV screen reporting on a husband's attempt to prevent his HIV-infected wife from having an abortion. I'd been engrossed for an hour or more in a waking revenge dream with a logistical flaw: how did I get the elevator doors open when there was no sign of the elevator?

Tom waited at the bottom of the bed in an ecstasy of expectation.

Chapter Ten

I CALLED JERRY a dozen times in two days and left four messages before I finally reached him.

"Oh yes," a light spacey voice said. "When did you want to come round?"

"Now."

"I'm sorry, I'm having to limit the chair to three bookings a day."

"Bookings? For what?"

"Haircuts."

"I'm Billy Phillips' brother. I'm trying to find out how he died."

"Oh yes," he said. "Then come in a couple of hours. I'm going to take a nap."

Jerry lived at the bottom of a hill four blocks behind General Hospital where Billy had died, in a one-sided dead end street of pastel-painted stucco houses. The front steps of his house faced the end of a wire-enclosed tunnel over the freeway. In a suburb of Minneapolis or New York, the houses in that street would have been owned by white collar families prudent with every penny. Here, sheets had been tacked over the windows and garbage was trampled into the sidewalk. San Francisco was the only North American city I knew where even the slum houses looked pretty.

The man who came to the door had knobby cheekbones and a manic smile and a rich purple bruise the size of a golf ball on the end of his nose, with similar stains on his neck and arms. His right eye was half closed and bloodshot as if he'd been punched. I had to force myself to pretend I really wanted to shake hands with him, because my initial reaction was not to touch him.

He motioned me from the front door directly into a living room where he kept an old barber's chair with chipped enamel and large metal cabinets sparsely lined with supplies of shampoo and conditioners. The rest of the furniture was strictly functional and secondhand, except for a living Christmas tree in a corner, still decorated with colored lights blinking on and off.

"Isn't it pretty?" Jerry asked me, scratching at one of his arms.

"Yes," I said automatically, then checked myself and searched his face for irony, which wasn't there. His good blue eye brightened as he stood watching the blinking lights.

"A cup of coffee?" he asked. "A glass of wine? A little thorazine or nembutal?"

"Coffee," I said. But Jerry hovered around the living room, laboriously shifting professional size plastic bottles, picking up and reading three get well cards he'd arranged on the mantelpiece, glancing at me shamelessly to see if I'd noticed them.

"I'm sorry about the mess," he said. "I had to close my shop and move everything here when I got sick."

I sat on his couch and wondered what was the best way to introduce the topic of AIDS to someone who clearly suffered from it.

"I got your messages this morning," he said. "I was in the hospital overnight for a blood transfusion."

I touched my nose. "What is that?" I asked.

"You're from out of town," Jerry cried with a crazy kind of glee. "KS. Kaposi's Sarcoma. It's a cancer of the blood vessels that goes with AIDS. Nobody knows why some of us get this and some of us get the pneumonia, though KS cases are going down. It's the disease of choice if you're lucky. Some people who only got KS are still alive six or seven years later." I heard about half of the little lecture he reeled off that day. I fill in the blanks now from all the times I heard the same information again.

While Jerry shuffled off to the kitchen I stared at a battered thrift store dining table and wondered what I was doing chasing another certain dead end in a shabby room in a city full of men who were sick. Then I cursed myself for being so empty, for having so little left to give after I tried to take care of myself.

He returned with a mug of coffee and a tube of prescription ointment. He sat beside me, scratched his arm again, and began smoothing the cream on the flaking skin. I thought of cells from his skin floating on top of my coffee and I gulped at it quickly before my imagination took over and I gagged.

"Do those hurt?" I asked.

"No," Jerry said. "They're called lesions and they don't hurt at all. Except my vanity. I've tried countless tubes of Clearasil and I'm here to tell you the claims in those advertisements you see are greatly exaggerated."

He was about my age, shorter, stocky despite his illness, with graying brown hair. His shirt and trousers were the grubbiest kind of wash-and-wear. He reminded me of Irish bartenders I had known. But he smiled and tried to keep his hoarse voice light, determined to amuse. "Nobody hit me in the eye. Although I sometimes deserve to be hit. I had an inconvenient lesion on my eyelid and another one in my throat but they removed them with a laser operation. I can tell when another lesion is starting. The place starts to itch."

"Did you know my brother?" I asked.

"Yes."

"Thank God," I said.

"I saw him once or twice. Do you know about the Healing Factory?" I shook my head. "They've taken over an old bathhouse South of Market for all kinds of faith healing shit. It's run by a street person called Marlin Golding. They interview him on television now."

"What would he know about Billy's death?"

"Your brother volunteered at a shelter Marlin Golding runs for AIDS patients off the streets. They call it the Dormitory. I went there a couple of times to donate haircuts and Billy was assigned to one of my clients. Something was wrong. You can tell by the way those people withdraw when you're not doing what they want. Billy was being shunned, and he was very troubled."

"What are they? A religious group?"

"They're shit off the street who are onto a good thing," Jerry said lightly. "At least that's what I think."

"When was the last time you saw Billy there?"

"Eight or nine months ago. Before I got sick." He paused,

concentrating on smoothing in the ointment until I showed puzzlement. "They wanted me to take the transfer just to do a couple of haircuts once or twice a month. The transfer is when they teach you how they want you to deal with the homeless clients." He added without looking at me: "You look like you need a haircut."

"Okay. Now?"

"I suddenly need to go to the bathroom," Jerry said, "and then I'll need to take another nap. It's like all the pain of being screwed and none of the fun. Noon on Monday."

"All right," I said, because I wanted to learn more.

Chapter Eleven

"MY USUAL SINUS," Luke said when I wondered if I'd got the right number. I caught myself worrying whether he was telling the truth: I was becoming suspicious about the health of every gay man I met.

"You sounded all right on the six o'clock news," I said. "Was your story taped earlier in the week?"

"Certainly not. I can always produce a voice for work."

"Do you have a minute to talk? I need some information."

"Sure," Luke said. I heard settling down noises and a slurp and swallow.

"What do you know about the Healing Factory?"

"Ah-ha! A lot. I did a series on AIDS organizations."

"Is what you know good or bad?"

"Good," Luke said. "A little off-the-wall, but no more than usual for this city."

"What I heard sounded like the People's Temple lives again."

"All that faith healing stuff? I think Marlin would like to be Jim Jones if he could, but they're downplaying all that now that they've become respectable. Marlin Golding was even written up in an editorial in the *Chronicle*."

"For healing AIDS patients?"

"Actually they never mentioned that. It was more like praising him for going from poverty to head of a moneymaking organization all inside a year. Death and Dying – San Francisco's dynamic growth industry." Luke hooted at his own joke.

"Actually they're performing a service that no one else has been willing to perform. About six years ago Marlin started these little meetings for AIDS patients in a room in a bathhouse that had closed for lack of business. The healing power of crystals and visualization, that kind of stuff. It's rampant in the Bay Area still and apparently quite legal. At least nobody seems to be thinking of taking anyone to court. Hundreds of AIDS patients follow one woman who sells self-healing tapes and books." Pause for a sip and swallow. "Marlin Golding's place came to be known as the Healing Factory. He started to get a reputation because a couple of his patients apparently went into remission, which actually did seem like a miracle then, because people knew far less about the course of the illness. Some PWAs get sick quickly and die quickly. Some get sick and stay sick but live for a year or two or more. And some people are diagnosed but after the first KS lesions or the first bout of pneumocystis they look and feel healthy for a long time, particularly with the new drugs. The families of a couple of men who seemed to get better gave Marlin quite a lot of money and he used it to start turning the bathhouse into a temporary shelter for homeless AIDS patients, just one night at a time. He got the bathhouse cheap because it was run-down and had a particularly sleazy reputation – there had been a fire there, and in 1981 a wealthy attorney" (Luke hooted at my expense) "was found dead in one of the rooms tied up in a sling with lots of unlikely objects stuck in his asshole. The family was able to hush it up because he apparently died of natural causes, a heart attack, but the place had to close down for six months. It reopened under a different name but the same owner and the same sleaze going on there. After it closed the second time for lack of business, just before all the remaining bathhouses were closed down by the city, nobody wanted to use it for anything, at least until people forgot what went on there."

I was determined to sound unshocked and nonjudgmental about the unnecessary details in Luke's story. "Isn't the city obliged to take care of homeless AIDS patients?" I asked evenly.

"The city funds the Dormitory now, although Marlin still puts in any private money he's given. The problem is that there are maybe 300 or 400 homeless street people with AIDS in San Francisco. The city has various hotels where it puts up homeless patients on three-day vouchers, and it even tried a small residential program in one hotel, but it doesn't have nearly enough rooms, and most places require a minimal standard of behavior. Catholic Charities opened a long-term residence for homeless patients in the Western Addition, but they only have room for about 40 people, and they have to go through evaluation at General."

Luke clearly did his homework: I was forced to revise my opinion of him as another TV reporter who kept nothing in his head except worries about how his hair looked.

"The Episcopal Sanctuary took over another bathhouse to house the homeless, but they won't take AIDS patients if they're intoxicated." I heard Luke take another swallow. "Marlin's Dormitory attracts the people with nowhere else to go. Not just the socially marginal white gay men who are too difficult for the regular AIDS service agencies and clinics to handle, but the IV drug users and winos that alcoholic treatment centers can't handle." Luke paused for a hefty swallow. "The population that's most at risk for contracting AIDS now are the black and Latino IV drug users. The Health Department's AIDS Office and the AIDS service agencies were burned by criticism that they're run by and geared to helping gay white men. So it was logical to fund the Dormitory, which seemed to be able to win the trust of gay and straight street people and IV drug users whether they're black or Hispanic or white. It's a front lines operation. I think they still have one or two deaths on the premises every week, though Marlin has a staff person now who evaluates the needs of the clients who come there and tries to channel them towards the more traditional agencies."

"You really mean that the San Francisco Health Department is funding an operation which pretends to heal AIDS patients by faith?"

"No, no. The Factory's activities are completely separate from the Dormitory. The Factory is more of a consciousness raising group now with no mention of faith healing. And Marlin uses any money that's donated at the meetings to help the work at the Dormitory."

"Billy volunteered there," I said.

"Who told you?" Luke said.

"An AIDS patient I ran into."

"Did you get any help at The Dating Game?"

"No," I said, too lazy to explain what had happened. "But this man seemed very negative about Marlin Golding."

"Go to the Sunday morning meeting and judge for yourself," Luke said. "It's open to everyone."

"I intend to."

"Listen," Luke said. "A percentage of AIDS patients suffer from organic brain damage, which I suppose can take the form of paranoia. Also there's more anger around AIDS than around anything else I know of. It's a matter of life and death, and people get terribly jealous of anyone who has more power than they do, or who seems to be helping more, or who's healthier even."

"I'm sure you're right," I said. I was feeling more alert as Luke sounded more blurred. It was late at night and I felt lonely and let down as Luke's attention slipped away. "I have some comments on your city and then I'll let you go. I've found a way to tell who's gay and who's straight. The gays drop their eyes to my crotch when I'm out running. They never do it until they're close up, and then suddenly the eyes drop. I was running on Kennedy Drive and another runner was staring so hard he tripped and fell as he passed me."

Luke roared. "Did you help him up?"

"I kind of stopped at a distance and signalled at him was he all right. He got very red-faced and scowled at me."

"Male bounce and jiggle," Luke said with enthusiasm. "Running shorts are the sexiest clothes in the world. They're just an excuse for genital display. Don't tell me straight men don't know exactly how much they're showing."

"We might think about it, but it's considered bad form to talk about it at length," I said. "Also, something I've noticed in the Castro. I was walking past Orphan Andy's and there was this couple. The man had AIDS, I'm sure, because he looked emaciated, and he was talking to this older woman. She was listening really intently, and she had her arm outstretched on the table, reaching towards him but not touching him. Then two minutes later I passed Without Reservations and there were two men sitting in the window." Luke roared; he seemed to know what was coming. "I know the older man definitely had AIDS because he had KS marks on his arms. The other man was much younger, and he didn't look sick, but he was listening really intently, and his arm was on the table in exactly the same position as the woman's, reaching towards the other man but not touching him."

"They were emotional support volunteers from the Shanti Project," Luke said. "They counsel AIDS patients. They do role-plays as part of their training, and the two volunteers were copying exactly what had been demonstrated. It's meant to show the clients that the counselors are physically available if the clients want to be touched for comfort, but at the same time they aren't going to touch first in case the clients feel threatened by physical contact."

"All right," I said. "I'll let you go. One more thing. There's a bag in Billy's bathroom with about 50 condoms in it. Are they giving them away one hundred at a time?"

"He probably picked them up at the bathhouses while they were still open," Luke said. "You ought to find yourself a woman."

"I don't know how," I said, then tried to joke: "Are there any straight women left in San Francisco?"

"Two pieces of advice about the city," Luke said. "Don't take the underground Muni during business hours if you're in a hurry. It breaks down all the time, particularly at rush hour in the financial district. And never *never* take the 24 bus. They beat up any single man who might be a faggot. Goodnight."

Chapter Twelve

IT'S TRUE I went to the Sunday morning meeting at the Factory looking for corruption because it seemed to be the only place to look. The wide gray streets South of Market were baking to dust under a hot sun, with few signs of life in the buildings – auto repair shops, furniture warehouses, wooden alleys of four-story barricaded apartment houses with their bright paint flaking. A handful of black women gathered outside a cream-colored Roman Catholic church with two gilded domes; the pink Templo Calvario next door looked boarded up.

The Factory was a low wooden building between a body shop and an abandoned bread factory, hidden from the main road around the corner of a courtyard. A mile away at the eastern end of the industrial street skeletons of new high rises scratched the sky on the southern edge of the financial district. I noted that the freeway overpass was only three blocks west of the Factory, with low green hills beyond.

You entered the courtyard through a door in a high black iron gate with a dark blue sign. It read in yellow letters:

THE HEALING FACTORY
FOR THE AIDS LOVE FLAME

—

DORMITORY

—

MARLIN M. GOLDING, DIRECTOR

The courtyard was just a space, a dark concrete path between brick walls leading to the open door of the Factory, which looked like the entrance to the offices of a light industrial building. Directly inside the wooden doorway a steep narrow staircase covered with hard reddish carpet led up to another open doorway. So far I'd seen no one and heard nothing. As I climbed the stairs an office came into view; I saw safe deposit boxes behind a thick glass partition with a trough in the counter under the glass for money transactions. A handwritten sign was taped to the glass: "All pockets must be emptied. Contents returned to you on leaving." But the office was empty.

I walked through the second door into an empty hallway. To the left was an archway backed by a mirror in which I saw myself, though I looked away immediately; the mirror was flanked by the beginnings of two flights of stairs. To my right, more flights of red-carpeted stairs. Facing me was another archway. As I moved towards it I began to hear movement and voices.

I paused at the top of a wider flight of stairs inside a large basement room. Long rows of lockers faced me at the bottom against the opposite wall. At first sight the space beneath me to the right resembled the lounge of a vacation hotel. In the farthest corner there was a carpeted platform scattered with large cushions. Palm trees and ficuses between the stairs and the platform half-hid a sunken rock garden with a small still pool. Tall clay jars with bird of paradise stalks and bowls of less exotic flowers filled the spaces between the trees. The rest of the room was lined with empty rows of folding chairs. I was early. Almost all the handful of men and women who sat waiting in an official kind of hush smiled at me when I reached the bottom of the stairs.

The room was windowless, even high on the walls at street level, and the lighting obviously kept low for effect. Some electric light leaked from the corridor I'd come from and another corridor behind the rows of chairs. The wall behind the palms glowed from dim spotlights. But the main light was candlelight: lit candles everywhere, red pillars that smelled of artificial strawberry essence, though the smoke didn't mask another smell I'd been trying to identify ever since I'd entered the building. It was the sour-sweet smell of urban decay, but a more specific memory of that smell nagged me.

Taped New Age music, evocative of trees or seas or the wind, nonspecific and sentimental, haunted that basement room. As I hesitated in front of the rows of chairs, I recognized the perfectly circular rock garden for what it was: a drained Jacuzzi, its sides disguised with moss and ferns. Then I remembered the smell, I guess because a Jacuzzi is one of the stale excuses for taking off your clothes in pornographic movies when the actors are playing innocent. The Healing Factory smelled like the Times Square porno movie house I used to go to when I was too drunk to waste my money on a whore.

I sat in one of the back rows, as close as I decently could to where two of the most beautiful women I'd ever seen were sitting with a young man. At first I thought they were twins because they had the same pale blonde hair and light blue eyes that seemed to attract a lot of what light there was in the room. But one woman was definitely older, a little more withdrawn or resigned. The man sat between them in a kid's flannel lumber jacket, the skin on his face transparent, his teeth chattering as he folded his arms over his gut.

"I'll see if I can find something to put over you," the older woman said in distress, and walked off into the corridor behind us.

"They must have blankets somewhere," the woman who was left told the young man, and caught my eye.

"At least left over from the last incarnation of this building," I said.

"They didn't have blankets when it was a bathhouse," the young man said, "just sheets." His voice was close to a weak wail of pain.

"They have blankets in the Dormitory," the woman told me, "but those rooms are completely closed off. It seems to be a different operation. I'm Kay Hawkes and this is my brother George." I felt that I could read her mind. She was strong enough to set aside her pain and smoothly proceed with all the business of getting her dying brother through the day. I couldn't take my eyes off her.

The other woman returned empty-handed, and introduced herself as Harriet, George's other sister. Everything was locked up.

"We don't have to stay," Kay told her brother, who was bent over and groaning. "We can call Dave and Gary and ask them to pick us up now." I'd already confirmed that both women wore wedding rings.

"I want to wait and see Mar," George said unhappily. He leaned sideways and rested his head in Kay's lap, but he couldn't get comfortable and soon sat up again.

"I'm going to bring blankets next time," Harriet said.

Someone came out of the corridor behind us and headed across the room. It was Jerry. When he sat down I signalled to him but I had trouble getting his attention. Then he turned and stared at me without recognition. I caught movement out of the corner of my left eye and turned to see Jerry hobbling down the main staircase. He reached the bottom and turned towards us. His face was as bloated and cheerful as the face of the man in the moon. Before the morning was over I saw two more men who looked alike. Which is how I learned that in its advanced stages KS casually discards individual differences.

A scrawny young black man, maybe 23 years old, a friend of George's, came and sat in front of him, turning a chair to face us.

"How are you, Adrian?" Kay asked.

"Too young and pretty to die," Adrian said.

"That's my line," George mumbled, brightening grudgingly.

"I am going to eat and sleep right," Adrian announced, "and introduce no more toxic waste into my system and I am going to prevail."

"You have a wonderful attitude," Kay said, with no irony at all. She turned to me again, briefly searching my eyes, perhaps to find out where I fitted. I can't have looked much healthier than another man who sat down near us: he had short dark hair and a trim body, though his facial skin was a peculiar red that might have been due to a badly-managed suntan. Or perhaps Kay lost no opportunity to draw a newcomer into her circle, never knowing where unexpected benefits would come from: a friend in need, news of a treatment that would ease George's pain.

The room filled quickly now, and although I stayed conscious of Kay close to me I couldn't take my eyes off the men and women who'd come here in the hope of holding onto life. A short blond frail man in a three-piece gray suit nodded a cheerful good morning to everyone around him, then pulled papers out of his briefcase and began highlighting them. He looked like the plucky clerk in a Masterpiece Theater adaptation of a Dickens novel, forced by propriety to spend more on clothes than on food. Another young man had the limited but extreme facial repertoire of a Keystone Kop, a black moustache and bushy eyebrows framing bright doleful eyes. "I feel like shit," he announced, and his eyes started to water, then he chuckled at himself. A shaggy street person with blotched scarred skin, his body reduced and crumpled, ostentatiously pulled the hood of his sweat shirt over his head and withdrew into himself to attract attention. A man who must have been over 70 smiled at the Keystone Kop and stayed tolerant of the street person sitting two chairs away. He had white hair and a lined face and wore clothes never intended to be more than functional, that signaled no indications of his sexual preference. A man in his late 20's adjusted loose pastel clothes over a *Gentleman's Quarterly* body. Four or five of the men signalled a young black woman with her hair in silver cornrows to come and sit beside them. Another woman, round-faced and overweight in a crumpled smock, worked harder for attention, moving up and down the rows and asking acquaintances for news and hugs. A short man with thinning brown hair and a leg that dragged fussed around his overweight and pouting male companion.

Another couple began descending the stairs: an old woman in her Sunday best eased herself down sideways one step at a time, her body turned to see how her companion was managing. When I saw him I felt trivial. His head was as hairless and featureless as an embryo's. I suppose it was chemotherapy that had stripped his skin of all signs of growth and ageing. The pink nakedness of his face made him seem vulnerable and tender, but he was truly unreadable.

After they sat down the woman hovered over him, frowning and clucking.

"Oh mother," he said, "you're wearing perfume. You know how I hate that perfume."

Chapter Thirteen

THE FIRST TIME I saw Marlin Golding I almost laughed out loud, at him and at myself for hoping to find evil in him. I noticed him out of the corner of my eye, some kind of colorful toy, then my head jerked back because I wasn't sure what I'd seen. He walked slowly down the stairs, a foot hovering over every step in a parody of a religious or official procession, his carriage and profile ridiculously solemn. At first I thought he was a painted dwarf, because the man who lumbered one step above him was a foot-and-a-half taller and a mass of muscle. Marlin was a ragbag of color: a purple caftan down to his calves, a few inches of loose green pants showing underneath, and his wispy brown hair painted in long stripes of primary colors a quarter inch wide and pulled into a neat multicolored knot nearly as big as the back of his head. A large gold cross swung from his thin white neck; gold earrings glinted in both ear lobes. Later I noticed that he wore a thick gold wedding band. I never discovered which of his unions it symbolized.

Marlin could have begun the meeting by walking into the room and ringing a bell. That slow unannounced descent was risky, a test of how much presence he had. I can't have been the only man in the room who was ready to find him ridiculous: some of the men with AIDS sitting in that room came from walks of life where a man like Marlin would have trouble getting into people's homes. I suppose it was easy to make allowances for Marlin when they had to face more desperate decisions. His entrance eventually achieved its intended effect. Voices dropped away, and most eyes focused on him as he reached the bottom of the stairs and turned right to cross the room. Some men smiled openly at him, but for attention, hoping to be acknowledged. He stared straight ahead, apparently self-absorbed, although I think I caught him trying not to show how pleased he was to establish the importance of himself and the occasion he'd created. The blond muscleman still followed one step behind, not knowing what to do with his hands or arms or eyes. He seemed grateful to settle into the background when Marlin finally reached the carpeted stage and folded himself with self-conscious grace into a lotus position facing the audience.

Heads craned, except for a few that were too weighted with pain or expected the miracle to come to them. Marlin took his time, eyes closed, praying or meditating or pretending, while we waited. The music tried to evoke windy star space, something like that. The genuine flames of 40 scented candles made graceful attempts to climb the air, supple and serene as world class athletes going through their routines.

Marlin raised his head and addressed the room spaciously. "Welcome to the Healing Factory for the flame that heals AIDS with love," he cried. His voice was high and thin with nerves or self-induced drama. "Please take part in our service, all of you," he called, "whatever your reasons for being here this morning. Remember that the power of love multiplies infinitely. If you pray for yourself, one person may be healed. If we all pray for each other, that prayer may leave this room like a gentle fire and heal the entire city."

Marlin's words were simple and powerful, but at first his ambitions were subverted by his voice. Marlin had trouble talking. His words ran together or halted between syllables. He'd begin a sentence like a cultivated man and trip over an ordinary vowel, then try to cover up with a sudden rush of emotion. Until he calmed down I was bewildered by all the echoes I traced in his voice: of a Buddhist chant and a Muslim call to prayer, or Hollywood's portrayal of them, with maybe an underlying educated Southern accent or an attempt at one. You had to listen hard to hear what he was saying. But everyone seemed to be listening.

"We have seen miracles in this room," Marlin called. "Men suffering from an illness the doctors say is always terminal who are well today and have stayed well for years. There's no secret to the miracles that have occurred here. As human beings we have the power and the right to heal ourselves. It's sickness that is out of place in the universe. All we do at the Healing Factory is allow the serenity and wellness of the universe to inhabit and heal our bodies. Any scientist will gladly explain to you the scientific basis of what we do here. Remember, as we visualize and create the love flame healing our bodies, that our central nervous systems don't distinguish between real and imagined events. Our central nervous systems know that the flame we think we only visualize healing our bodies is real, and that is one of the reasons miracles occur in these rooms."

Marlin closed his eyes and settled into himself again for another two or three minutes. I thought I felt irritation in the room. Maybe the patients who were in physical pain wished that Marlin would get on with it; maybe the men in business suits were angry that their humiliating disease had brought them to this. But the need in the room was so great that at first I thought: "Why not? What harm can this do?" I glanced at Kay as she glanced at her brother. There were no doubts in her face, just hope that Marlin's message was making George feel better. Harriet sat bent over, chin in hand, tears running unchecked down her face.

"I want everyone here to choose a candle flame they can concentrate on easily," Marlin called. "Watch the flame for a few moments. Appreciate its beauty. Appreciate its power. Recall that it is one of the elements of the universe to which you belong. Flame created you. You will move into flame when you die and you will be reborn in flame when we all mingle and meet again as one. The flame is you. Beauty and power. Pure power without pain. Beginning now, inhale the flame through your nostrils, very slowly. As you breathe in the flame expand your chest. The flame continues to flow, filling the middle of your lungs. Raise your shoulders and collarbone. You've made room for the flame to fill your lungs completely. Hold the flame within you. Now that you have enabled the flame, it will take over. The flame is in your blood, traveling instantly and secretly to every part of your body, secretly devouring pain, secretly and relentlessly consuming sickness. Hold the flame inside you for another second. Slowly, begin to exhale the flame through your nostrils. Watch the flame flow from your nostrils and return to the candle. Draw in your abdomen to help the flame empty your body of impurity. Slowly drain the flame from your body. Now that your body is empty, wait. Consider that you and the flame are now one. When you inhale the clean pure flame again, you will become pure cleansing flame. Your body will be reborn. You will be healed."

I probably had an easier time breathing Marlin's flame than some of the others in the room. I'd seen a similar relaxation exercise, minus the flame, in a running magazine and tried using it to visualize faster running, although I got distracted after five minutes. I went along with everyone else at the Factory that morning and breathed Marlin's flame twenty times until I was light-headed and calm and full of goodwill. Of course the flame wouldn't heal AIDS, but it might make a patient feel better for a day, even alleviate stress enough to briefly halt the progress of the disease. The pain in the room had certainly eased. The audience was hypnotized.

I was hypnotized and didn't realize it until I saw that the rest of the room was in motion. Three or four men in brightly colored T-shirts came and stood next to Marlin in front of the stage, and the audience began forming lines in front of them. When I joined Marlin's line it was shorter than the others. I noticed a few men grinning sheepishly because they'd rushed to join the line in front of Marlin then found that nearly everyone was lining up democratically in front of his assistants. The men at the front placed their hands on each person's temples and gazed into their eyes. No words seemed to be exchanged. I noticed that the faces of the men at the front all looked alike. They were all Caucasian, of different ages and coloring and physique, but they looked as if they'd had a strip of calm pasted across their faces between eyebrows and nostrils. The skin in that area of each of their faces even looked lighter and less lined. *Like the skin I touched on Billy's temple when he was already dead* . Their eyes were uniformly warm and soft and unfocused. I looked around. Everyone else in varying degrees had that calm around the eyes, even the old woman with her son directly ahead of me. But her softened eyes were still alert as she tried to hold her concern in check to keep the distance her son demanded. She turned and looked up at me with a lively interest, smiling wryly, indicating that she wanted to be friends.

Standing behind the reddened egg of the man's head in front of me, I saw Marlin's small hands reach up and touch the temples. Then the man bent down and Marlin's arms appeared around his shoulders. He kissed the man's neck lightly and clung for a moment. I stared into Marlin's eyes looking up at me. His plain little face was lightly tanned and moist with some kind of lotion. His eyes were large and brown and continually melting. I looked elsewhere. The man in front of me slipped away. Marlin dealt with the mother more perfunctorily. Then he reached up and touched my head lightly. I forced myself not to cringe. For a moment his eyes focused and met mine, but as soon as we connected his eyes began to melt again. I couldn't help taking it personally. I snickered. Something flickered in Marlin's eyes; he blinked and stared at me, without warmth now, and I moved away from him.

The crowd drifted into a locker room behind the main room where there were tables set up with wine and apple juice and fruit. Harriet had slipped away as the meditation ended, I guessed to find out if the husbands had arrived with transport. George was so concentrated in conversation with a small group of friends that for a moment I imagined an unbroken lifeline holding their bodies together. I went up to Kay, who waited nearby. She looked sad. We searched each other's eyes to find out what the other thought of what went on at the Factory, although her search was more accepting and less urgent than mine.

"Do you have a relative who's ill?" she asked.

"No. I had a brother who volunteered here. He didn't have AIDS, but he died anyway." Which established that we were on the same side in the room's division: those who would die soon, and those who loved the dying or the dead, and would have given much to keep them alive.

"Does this help your brother?" I asked Kay.

She thought about it, then gestured at the feeling in the room. "It's very peaceful here. I think George feels that peace after he leaves."

"Do you think Marlin cures people?" I asked.

"I've been told about some incredible remissions that are very hard to explain any other way," she said. I think she meant: I would believe anything now, even if it would previously have insulted my reason and my intelligence, if it would only help George live without pain for just another day.

Harriet appeared at the top of the stairs looking for an opportunity to signal. I drew Kay's attention to her, away from me. There was a man with Harriet who looked and dressed like me. I knew with certainty what he felt: that being here was a duty which he hoped to perform with grace, although he'd rather be almost anywhere else. Kay found her brother and told him they could go. While George said his good-byes I watched Kay looking up at the man at the top of the stairs. I saw her clear-eyed gratitude when she met the eyes of a man who shared a life she relied on. I felt the old glass wall rise around me, shutting me off from a world where I looked like an inhabitant but could never belong. Kay and I said goodbye and wished each other luck. George ignored me.

The conversations I overheard around me were about critical or final things that had to be dealt with on a daily basis: tests and symptoms and the side effects of experimental drugs and alternative therapies that had helped a lot of people, and the realization by certain men that there was almost nothing left for them to try. The man in the three-piece suit chatted to the chemo patient as if they were discussing exhibits at an opening. I caught the old woman watching me very deliberately.

"My name is Imogen Brown," she said. "Do you have a son with AIDS?"

"I have no children," I said. "Is that your son?"

"My son Frank," she said ruefully. "I have four sons and none of the rest of them have AIDS nor are they likely to get it. Frank is the one I've always been closest to because he's the only one who still lives in San Francisco. I was three years old during the San Francisco earthquake. I survived the earthquake and it looks as if I'm going to survive AIDS." She had slight aphasia, running some words together and balking at others; I assumed she'd suffered a slight stroke. She looked at me with what seemed to be amused exasperation; maybe old age foreshortened emotion. "What do *you* think of the Factory for the healing flame for AIDS?"

"Not much," I said involuntarily, and realized how much I meant it. Her sharp eyes had cleared away some of my guilty hedging.

"I don't either," Imogen said. "Every time I tried to hold my breath I started choking. But I suppose if it helps any of these poor men." I looked around for Marlin. Imogen was even quicker than me at leaving before she outstayed her welcome. "I'm in the phone book if you ever feel like visiting," she said.

I thanked her. Marlin had joined his audience, moving quickly from one person to the next with a kind of preening graciousness. Two or three times I heard a sound that surprised me, a cackle that didn't seem to be echoed by the patients he was talking to. I suppose you might call it graveyard humor. I put myself in his path and introduced myself.

"I know who you are," Marlin said, and paused, his voice husky and insinuating.

But I showed no surprise.

"I was sorry to hear about your brother's death. I wish I'd known him better the short time he worked here." His accent in regular conversation was fairly consistently neutral, his manner rather calculating and professional; his eyes were now merely poised to melt.

"I'd like to see as much as possible of what Billy's life was like towards the end," I said. "I'd like to come to the Dormitory one night and watch the work you do."

"I'm afraid I can't allow that," Marlin said with some enjoyment. "Our clients may be destitute, but we feel they still have a right to privacy and anonymity."

"I think that's a wonderful attitude," I said. "I want to give money to some organization in Billy's memory, and of course I want to know exactly what I'd be giving the money to."

"Call Shannon," Marlin said, glancing around to see where he would move next. "She's in charge of running the Dormitory and she could see you one afternoon before the clients start to arrive."

"I will," I said. "You must spend a fortune on candles."

There was never any room in the bed. Whatever positions we started in, Tom always ended up sleeping in the middle with me pushed to either side trying to get away from him because he was a hot weight that added to the discomfort of the night. My

74

behavior didn't make sense to me; three or four times a night he'd get up and move of his own accord, but I couldn't bring myself to move him to make room for myself.

I tried to jerk off thinking about fucking Kay, but it didn't work. I ended up holding her in my arms and talking about what had happened during an imaginary day. I found I wasn't very good at invention.

Chapter Fourteen

JERRY'S EYES LIT up and he reached out to touch a mark on my arm. I pulled back angrily.

"It's an insect bite I scratched," I said, covering the scab with my hand so that he couldn't get near it. I thought: He wants everyone to have his disease. He doesn't want to be alone.

He stood in front of me and pointed his comb at me. "Give me a definition of utter chaos," he said.

"Your clients lining up to get haircuts while you stand there telling jokes."

"Very good," he said. "But I space my clients these days so that I can tell as many jokes as I want."

He looked sicker today. The purple patches on his face had shrunk and faded, but he was tired and very slow, and his left foot dragged badly when he walked.

"I want a definition of total chaos before I do another thing," he said.

"Tell me."

"Father's Day in Oakland," he said. His face lit up and he started giggling to himself. "How do you get a gay man to stop fucking?"

"Start an AIDS epidemic?" I suggested.

"It's quicker and easier just to marry him," Jerry said. "I can vouch for the truth of that from my last boy friend. Who incidentally was the one I think gave me AIDS."

"You're a racist sexist pig," I said without conviction.

"But funny," he said. "Be careful." He waved his comb at me.

"It's not wise to fool with a pushy hairdresser. You may end up with half your head the way you want it and the other half the way I want it."

I growled.

"Why do lesbians marry each other?"

"Shut up, Jerry." I glared at him. "I'm a former kneejerk liberal. That means I have hardly any sense of humor except at my own expense."

"So that they can hold hands and block the sidewalk," he insisted on telling me.

"Okay, enough of this frivolity. Follow me to the kitchen and I'll wash your hair."

There was an aquarium above the kitchen sink with one bloated unhappy goldfish. Jerry introduced me to it and told me the names of his cats, who were not around. I'd been dreading the moment I felt his swollen hands on my head, and trying to convince myself it was because Jerry was so generally grubby. But the first touch of his fingers was tempered by the warm water. I almost began to enjoy being touched. God knows my body was starved for any human contact. The warmth and comfort on my head made it easy to think: We share the same destiny, we get sick, we grow old, we die.

It was an effort for Jerry to finish towelling my hair. When we went back to the living room he had to sit down to rest on the living room couch. "It's getting harder to get through the day," he said, keeping it light, chuckling at his predicament.

"Do you depend on cutting hair to pay the bills?" I asked.

"I get $600 a month SSI," Jerry said.

"Is that what AIDS patients are expected to live on?"

"That's what all disabled patients are expected to live on if they don't have private disability insurance," he said. "But all my haircuts are under the table. As far as the government's concerned I'm too sick to work."

I stopped myself from looking around the room and took it in from memory so that he wouldn't see what I was thinking: He has nothing to sell and I'm sure he has no savings; when he does get too sick to work he won't be able to pay the rent.

"Let's get this show on the road," Jerry said. "Let's make you sexy so that all the gay men will want to tell you what happened to your brother."

"I'm going to tell Luke Carroll he should do a story on the economics of being an AIDS patient," I said.

"He already did, years ago," Jerry said. "So did every TV station and newspaper in the country by now. How come you never noticed before?"

"Why do you get so little?"

"We already get more than other patients," Jerry said. "People with cancer are *jealous* of us because we have so many volunteer organizations and because we've organized so much publicity and lobbying. How is Luke Carroll?"

"Fine," I said. "Totally ambitious."

"Is he still working full-time?" Jerry asked.

"Sure. Isn't he full-time at the station?"

"I wondered how his health was doing," Jerry said, cutting.

I felt the beginning of a certain dread. "What about his health?" I asked.

"Didn't you know Luke Carroll has AIDS?" Jerry asked blithely, cutting away.

I moved my head to look at him and he stopped, barely trying to conceal the delight of the bringer of sensationally bad news. "You're mistaken," I said. "Luke Carroll is as healthy as I am."

"Then you're in bad shape," Jerry said. "Luke is the most famous AIDS patient in San Francisco."

I allowed myself to think thoughts I'd kept hidden beneath the deadening depression I'd suffered since Billy's death: This thing is too big for any of us. It's like the end of the world.

Jerry chattered on. "He was working for Channel 7 when he was diagnosed a year ago and they let him do a big story on what it felt like. I don't think they had much choice. A television station could hardly fire one of its reporters who got AIDS, particularly a station that gay activists had accused of homophobia. Luke was a spectacular opportunity to clean up their act and win the gay audience. Since then he's on the air twice as much as he used to be. They'll probably try to get Pavarotti for the memorial service."

Jerry went on talking, but what he said sounded more and more unreal. I remembered what Luke had told me about AIDS dementia. Maybe Jerry was embroidering uncontrollably on a rumor. I wished he'd stop talking.

"I can't take this," I said. "Please finish cutting my hair."

"Welcome to San Francisco," he said.

I didn't bother to look in the mirror he offered me when he finished. I let him charge me $40 and another $20 for a large bottle of coal tar shampoo. I didn't realize how short my hair was until that afternoon when I ran past a school yard and two kids yelled "Faggot!" Only a wire fence saved them from my rage.

Chapter Fifteen

DOWN AT THE bottom of the stairs people came knocking at the front door in the middle of the night. The cat jerked against me and I was awake and listening. No one needed me at three in the morning. The knocking turned to hammering on the glass. Then the shouting started, an ugly howl, a raspy hurled monosyllable I couldn't decipher. I'm sure it woke the street, and perhaps it was intended to; an insult and a challenge to show us how little we could order what happened to us. Or else the man who howled had left the rest of us too far behind to care what we thought of him. Then I heard noise on the stairs. Even as I jumped up I realized it was someone hurrying down the stairs next door. A door opened. There was a conversation, inquiries that sounded relatively friendly, but shouted, though the speakers were standing on the same doorstep.

When the hammering started regularly in the middle of the night I learned to identify it as soon as I woke up and go right back to sleep. Sometimes not. I'd taken the banging front room door off its hinges and put it at the back of a closet, but the apartment was full of noises and surprise. There was a tall window at the top of the long first flight of stairs. When I first heard noise at the front of the house I thought it was Tom boxing a supermarket paper bag, but I found him in his hiding place at the back of the bookcase. I discovered that the window above the stairs was open under the blind, and too high for me to reach without a tall stepladder. The blind flapped in a breeze; a strong enough wind crossed the landing and flapped the louvered swing doors of the closet where I'd stacked the blinds I'd taken off the front and back windows. I wanted light in that apartment.

One night I thought I heard a rat in the kitchen. Next day, behind another spare door leaning against the kitchen wall, I discovered a second door leading from the kitchen, but barred from opening inwards by a heavy wooden bolt secured in iron sockets. From the inside it was easy to slide out the bolt. When I opened the door I found an empty aviary at the top of a dusty outside staircase built into the core of the house. I closed the door and replaced the bolt. It seemed to me there was no way the door could be opened from outside. I still felt vulnerable.

Sometimes a ghetto blaster would be turned on full volume below me. It was as if someone was finely tuned to the extent of my patience; just when the sound began to be intolerable it was turned down or off. I heard words of conversation, mostly at night, borne suddenly out of total silence through the walls or floors; it was impossible to tell whether the sounds came from the tenants below or next door. If the sound was loud enough for me to hear, it was an argument, except once, when a woman screamed on and on in a relentless fuck.

I was waiting in the airless room for Luke to return my call. The house that had been quiet began to ring and shake with a fight that spewed from nowhere.

"I never did nothing to you!"

"Shut your fucking mouth bitch!"

She screamed as she was thrown against a table or chair or tripped over it. Furniture toppled and skidded. Or he hit her with the furniture. She went on shrieking back at him as he accused her. Only the garbage names he called her made it through the walls, not what he accused her of. The fight quieted to fragments of a heartsick conversation. Then he started to shout and blame her again and she screamed as he hit her.

I thought it would never stop. I dialled 911 and told the police that a woman was being beaten up and gave them the address. "What is your name?" I hung up.

I thought, sick to my bones, that I'd never enter their lives, I wouldn't place myself in the path of their violence to rescue anyone: I'd worked too hard at leaving brute violence behind me, I'd come too close to returning to it. I realized that there were limits to what I'd do to find out how Billy died. I'd assumed I was dealing with people who had something to lose, who couldn't risk erupting in the light of day. I'd assumed I was dealing with people who thought more or less like me, to whom murder was an act of desperate resort, to be plotted and hidden. If Billy had been killed casually, by people who lived every day a gunshot or knife wound this side of dying, I had no weapons to deal with it.

Chapter Sixteen

LUKE CAME TO the door wineglass already in hand, looking sturdy and healthy but a little blurry, at least one joint down. He'd said he didn't like to go out to dinner because people stared at him. I took a bottle of white wine to show him that I really meant it when I said his drinking was his business, to show him I could be close to a bottle of booze and not have to drink it.

The moment I saw him I knew I was blocked, quite incapable of asking what I'd come to ask. It meant too much. He grinned at me as usual. I assumed it came naturally to him to be ingratiating; he'd learned early that it worked, so he used it when he could. I felt like a clumsy and uninformed intruder in the warm apartment with all the lights concentrated in the cheerful kitchen, the doors open to the night garden with its mysteries.

I stood in the kitchen watching Luke make pesto from scratch with five or six large cloves of garlic. "It cleans out the body," he said. "What did you want to talk about?"

"Did I say I had a topic?"

"You sounded urgent."

"I hope I don't need a reason to have dinner with you," I said, and noticed that I sounded almost flirtatious. "I wish I could have bought you dinner. I don't feel like cooking at Billy's apartment. Anyway I haven't cooked since I was a kid." I made myself shut up. Although I dreaded finding out what Jerry said was true, I knew from experience that the will to action would build up in me without my knowing until it exploded, and then I'd call Luke at two o'clock in the morning and ask him outright.

He looked at me with an amused keen interest which felt close to sexual. I think he thought I was uptight and square, but good-intentioned. "It really is embarrassing for me to eat out," he said. "Straight men ignore me but their wives or girl friends come over and say they just want to congratulate me for being so open and honest. Gays are the worst. They watch for me to do something they can trash me about. But you're a very businesslike man. I always assume you have an agenda."

I backed off and went to examine the framed diplomas hung next to the dining alcove, which was barely big enough for two. "Who's Barry Carroll?"

"Me," Luke said. "Barry Carroll sounds like a third-rate gay disc jockey. Worse, a third-rate straight disc jockey with strands of hair brushed sideways over his bald head. Have you noticed that gay men go bald more gracefully than straights?"

"I hadn't noticed that," I said.

"I named myself after Luke Skywalker. I think you'd be surprised how many gay men in San Francisco have changed their names. John became Zack, Henry became Chad. Vice presidents of banks moved here and became waiters South of Market and doctors opened flower shops. For a while we were the American dream in its purest form. We believed we could recreate ourselves endlessly."

"And then disaster struck," I said.

Luke smothered the pesto over two thick steaks of white fish and put them in the oven. "Dinner will be 12 minutes. It's cooler in the living room."

I sat on the sofa while he selected Gregorian chant for the stereo and *2001* for the VCR with the sound turned down to a rumor. I knew exactly why he'd chosen them: They were the coolest sight and sound for a heat wave night. He sat facing me, one knee on the cushion between us. I searched his face for a sign that he knew he was in mortal danger, and I couldn't find it. I believed he was strong, and a survivor.

Luke slurped his wine. I drank my cranberry juice.

"What did you think of the Factory?" he asked.

"I don't trust Marlin Golding," I said. "But I suppose what he does is harmless, a quick temporary fix. I do think it's a little strange it should be associated with the Dormitory that's funded with city money."

"The Dormitory is one of the most worthwhile projects in San Francisco."

"I'm going to see a woman called Shannon. So far she hasn't returned my calls."

"They're not the most organized people," Luke said.

For a while neither of us spoke.

"Those men singing," Luke said, nodding towards the stereo. "I wonder how many of them were gay? Did you ever go to the South Street Museum in New York?"

I shook my head.

"I went the first time I was in New York on vacation," Luke said. "There was an old restored sailing vessel still afloat. Down below they had blowups of old photos of groups of the sailors who'd sailed the Atlantic for weeks on that ship. I was looking at the pictures and thinking how young and ordinary they looked and how long they'd been dead. Their eyes were wide, maybe from the flash. Suddenly I thought: Some of those men loved each other. Whatever happened to them the rest of their lives, for some of them that love was the most important thing that ever happened to them. I felt that so clearly it seemed like a message from the dead."

I thought the unaccompanied voices of the men singing in praise was one of the most beautiful sounds I'd ever heard. I thought that I was used to knowing people who were easy to leave behind because they left nothing except memories, mostly bad, when I moved on. They were like me. I thought my memories of Billy were mostly good. My memories of Luke would be mostly good.

"What's wrong?" Luke asked, watching me in a hard challenging way.

I turned away and felt like a coward, so I had to look back at him. I was in great distress, but I cared enough about him to still wonder what he was feeling, how he managed to deal with it.

"Jerry the barber who cut my hair told me you have AIDS," I said in a rush, my eyes filling. Luke seemed to shrink. But he grinned at me. I felt against reason that although he'd been expecting my question, it confirmed to him that he was sick. Of course I knew what he was going to say.

"I do," he said, grinning shame-faced, meeting my eyes just long enough for self-respect then turning towards the video monitor where cold shapes lumbered smoothly in pure looking space.

I rushed in. "I guess I was the last person in the city to find out. I think I know why you didn't tell me." I saw Luke force himself to look at me. "You wanted to remember what it was like to deal with somebody who didn't know you have AIDS."

"That's right," he said. "Very good."

I added quickly, "If I —" and then stopped, unable to formulate what I wanted to say. I sat there, foolish. "You're so healthy."

"I am healthy," Luke said, glad to be given an opening. "My doctor found one KS lesion inside my butt a year ago – poetic justice, if you don't mind my saying so – and they zapped it with a laser. I've had no more lesions since and no other HIV diseases. My T-cell count is at the lower end of the normal range. I get a little tired sometimes, but that could be emotional. As far as I'm concerned I might as well not have AIDS."

"What can you expect?" I asked, trying to imply nothing disastrous.

"There are people alive who were diagnosed with KS seven years ago. For a lot of people now it's a question of maintaining their health with combinations of treatments until the final breakthrough."

"That's what Jerry said, though he looks really sick."

"A lot of men are still doing okay. Some of them claim not to have AIDS anymore. But they're outside the range of doctors' experience. AIDS hasn't been around long enough for doctors to have a natural history of the disease for really long-term patients. I never believed it was 100 per cent terminal like they used to say. I don't believe any disease is once you get a handle on it."

"You must have had this conversation with a hundred other people," I said.

"It's all right," Luke said. "It never seems to get boring. Unless they all happen on top of each other." I watched him and thought, he's strong and brave, and he can cope in ways beyond my imagining, but he shouldn't have to. It's beyond belief that this is happening to him.

"It's a gift," he said. He showed his teeth, waiting to see if I believed him. "Until I was diagnosed I had trouble getting on the air with gay stories more than once every other week. If *anyone* was to get AIDS it had to be me, because I had the chance to be the most visible person with AIDS in the city and the station had no choice but to back me. I'm pretty and viewers fall in love with me. I'm daily evidence that PWA's can go on working, and I'm a challenge to everyone who comes near me. Do they run away or do they believe the health authorities that nobody will catch anything from me? No restaurant or bar in the City would dare refuse to serve me, no landlord would refuse to rent an apartment to me, and other PWA's everywhere benefit from that."

Luke went to get the food from the kitchen. We ate the excellent fish and salad sitting on the living room floor because it was cooler there. It reminded me of when I was a student, or too drunk to sit up and eat, except that when I was drinking at home I was always alone.

The food made me optimistic. "What are your treatment options?"

"The only treatment I accept is aerosol Pentamidine to stave off the pneumonia," Luke said. "Why should I be a guinea pig? I feel fine and the experimental drugs I let them try on me all had horrendous side effects. They made me a lot sicker than I was before. I don't want to miss assignments because I'm too weak or nauseated. I have my blood chemistry monitored once a month and that's all."

I asked rashly: "How does it feel?"

"How does what feel?" he asked.

I said carefully, wishing I was somewhere else: "To know you have an illness that in many people turns out to be fatal."

"Jesus," Luke said in disgust, "don't turn into one of our San Francisco drama queens. We all die. What about TB and polio and the sleeping sickness epidemic between the two world wars that killed millions?"

"Nothing before attacked young men almost exclusively."

"What about the generation that died in Europe in the First World War?" Luke asked. "Tell that to the countries in Africa where AIDS attacks equal numbers of women and babies. Tell that to the infants in New York City who picked up the disease in their mothers' wombs. We all die. We're just the first generation that's made an industry out of our suffering. I'll tell you something – it doesn't seem real."

"That I already know," I said.

"It seems like a great pornographic fantasy. Sex and death, the two most important forces in the world, are suddenly locked in mortal combat. The porno movies I always loved were the ones where some butch number let us watch him getting his brains fucked out." Luke paid me enough attention to check for my reaction. I tried to look levelheaded and neutral, for Luke's sake, for Billy's sake. In fact I blocked out every image of a man being fucked in the ass that Luke tried to create for me.

"My two favorite porno superstars, Al Parker and Georgio Canale, both got fucked in their movies once or twice. You'd see them in dozens of movies giving it to one kid after another, then they lifted their own legs in the air. There used to be previews in the gay porno houses announcing that some star would finally take the big shaft in the ass in the next attraction. My favorite jerk off cassette is one where a muscleman takes it from one after another. That was the ultimate statement a man could make that he was gay. You'd see these hunks taking it at the tubs or at big parties South of Market and it meant that they weren't role posturing any more. They showed us who they really were. It was sort of like a woman losing her virginity. It wasn't something you could go back on. Then AIDS made getting fucked the truly ultimate act because thousands of men were dying because they did it. Even if it wasn't important to them when it happened, even if it was something they did over and over night after night with strangers, AIDS made it the most important act of their lives. I sit here at night jerking off over some really macho man taking it and it's sexy not only because he is defining himself, revealing himself to anyone who has the money to watch, but because it may truly be the most important act he ever commits, because it may kill him. We had so much sex that it stopped being important. Now it's important again."

Luke went to the kitchen for wine. He was still agitated when he came back, his forehead damp. He reached for the bag of grass. "Are you still with me?" he asked.

"I start checking out when you start talking about anal sex between men," I said carefully. "I just don't like to hear about it. But it's not that it's entirely alien to straights. I've had whores who were really into fingering my asshole. I think I even had an anal fantasy once. I was really drunk and unhappy and I put some cream on my asshole and stuck a finger up to see what it felt like. It might have been a drunken dream but I think I really did it."

"You're very conscientiously open-minded, aren't you?" Luke said.

"I was taught behavioral psychology at Minnesota and law at Columbia," I said. "It was an education free of values. And I had a gay brother. You know we all did talk about gayness a little bit in the early seventies. But I have to tell you that when I was playing with my butt I thought my life was shit anyway. I thought I'd end up on skid row and there was no way out. I was very badly demoralized."

"Like a bad trip at the tubs," Luke said.

I decided I'd better define some limits. "I would never do it with another man," I said. "I had enough polymorphous perversity when I was drinking. I want my life to be *less* complicated."

"I wasn't asking you," Luke said.

"I never said you were."

"Why is it straight men always think gay men are chasing them?"

"Because a lot of times you are. Billy told me he loved the idea of blowing straight men."

Luke grunted. "Your brother needed his consciousness raised. Did he ever have you?"

"Go fuck yourself."

Luke showed his teeth and watched the monitor.

What I liked most about him was his sharpness and his bright spirit. He never completely lost them, but they dimmed as he got higher towards the end of every evening we spent together. Even as Luke talked more, he became more essentially withdrawn. But he also grew more willing to be less the TV star.

"There's a Bette Midler song," Luke said. "'It's the heart afraid of dying that never learns to live.' Something like that. But it's the men who took the risks who are dying. It's the closet cases, the anal retentive assholes, the men who were scared to walk the alleys South of Market, who'll all still be alive 10 years from now. A whole generation of men who are dead defined themselves by who they wanted to fuck. Of course any red-blooded attractive gay man was going to fuck his brains out once he got the opportunity. You would too. Anything else is lesbian living."

"I don't think the song says living equals longevity," I said. "I've been trying to tell myself that Billy probably had hundreds of encounters that meant a great deal to him. That it doesn't matter that there don't seem to have been any long-term relationships in his life."

"Well I do make that equation between living and longevity," Luke said, suddenly harsh, "and so might you in my place. What I hate the most is that AIDS makes me feel as if we were worthless shit. It's as if we'd been singled out to suffer and die by the thousands because we don't count anyway, we're not part of the official dream."

"What gay men dying of AIDS are to America," I hazarded, "Africans dying of AIDS or hunger are to the world."

"Pretty good," Luke said.

"I still want to ask you something private. I feel like a voyeur, but I care about you. It's just that I was cut off from what went on inside people for so long that I don't know any longer if what we feel matches. What does it feel like to be told you might die?"

"Unreal," Luke said, and drank some wine. "First of all I hardly ever think about it because it gets in the way of all the things I want to do. A lot of the drama queens would say that's denial, but I don't think so. How can I live my life if I'm constantly thinking about dying? I certainly don't want a long series of last encounters. I'd get really sick of saying goodbye to people."

He glanced at me and saw me nodding but still waiting. "Sometimes when I'm alone in bed I get frightened," he said, sounding defiant. "Of stopping. Of being forced to let go before I want to. Being pulled away to nothing when I still want to be here. And we still carry those fearful old stories inside us. We don't really know it's nothing. One day in the Castro I was watching the fog roll in over the hills in the afternoon and I thought, I may never get to choose when I want to stop watching this. I may never get a chance to try and make it in Manhattan or L.A. But I don't think like that all the time. I don't care for the big thoughts of the grief industry. I think a lot of healthy people get involved in it because they need an excuse to cry over their own problems, get cheap thrills from other people's emotions."

"Sometimes when I'm feeling sorry for myself," I said, "I tell myself I'm lucky to be alive at all. It's a miracle I didn't get killed in the car. It's a miracle my liver didn't rot away."

"I always thought I was living on borrowed time," Luke said. "I was suicidal all through college and my first years in San Francisco. My heart stopped more than once in an emergency room. They'd release me from hospital in the morning and by the afternoon I'd be badgering somebody for an interview or a job. I thought once you were a star everything else fell into place. Which it did, sort of, because you can buy almost anything if you have the money."

"We're very alike," I said. "Do you have family?"

"I have parents in Philadelphia. They were finally starting to approve of me after my gay politicking and my bankruptcy. They were starting to enjoy me being a television star, they just wished I was a sportscaster."

"What –"

"They're coming out later in the summer for the first time ever. I suppose to mend the fences before it's too late."

We were both getting exhausted. "Do you have anybody, Luke?"

"A relationship? I hate that sentimental cow-eyed concept. There have been a string of men who bit the dust because I couldn't stand having them around. When a lover sits beside me and puts his arm around me I always want to move to the other side of the room. What about you? You're not exactly the typical head of a nuclear family."

"Being with someone is a habit I never learned. It's easier to go on being okay by myself than risk making things worse."

Luke sat up suddenly. "I'm going to crash. You can stay if you want to."

I looked blank, playing for time because I wasn't sure what Luke meant. He turned impatient. "You can sleep on the sofa or you can even have my bed if you want and I'll sleep on the sofa. We can have breakfast. Neither of us has to get up early."

"My sponsor promised to call me early from St. Paul," I said. Which was a lie.

I walked home in turmoil, snuggling into Billy's leather jacket for comfort. A damp high wind was doing its best to blow away the heat. Fire engines with their ugly noise barged across an intersection while I waited. I heard them every night as I lay in bed; if there had been real cause for all the alarms the entire city would be in flames.

At first I thought I was upset because it looked as if Luke was making a play for me. But that was the excuse I'd used not to stay with him. I knew how to say no. The trouble was that I still backed off from anyone who offered to get close, even Luke, who was in need, but would never admit it. And I had nobody else to care about.

Luke was immediate. Luke was in jeopardy. Luke reminded me of me. Unlike Billy, Luke was alive.

Chapter Seventeen

AS BILLY AND I got ready to go out for a burger we discovered that both of us had spent our share of the housekeeping money. We went upstairs to get more money from our mother. Maybe we were testing her because we wanted to believe she wouldn't fail us in the last resort; maybe she had money hidden and wanted to torment us; maybe we weren't always the prudent kids I remember us being and had spent carelessly that week. Our mother said there was no money left. I remember it as a shock that stopped us in our tracks, but it can't have happened that way. We knew when the money came from our father and from the county and we knew how much food was in the house because we bought it and cooked it, and now there was no food.

I remember our mother smiling at us standing there dumb-founded and turning scared. She had power over us after all. (Now I think she may have been ashamed and smiling with nerves.) We had no one to ask for money, no relatives we'd ever visited or heard our parents talking about, no family friends. We were always terrified to talk to the officials or caseworkers who handled our family in case they ended up separating us. We went downstairs. The worst part for me was watching Billy search cupboards and shelves for food because I didn't want him to be helpless. We ate corn flakes for dinner. (I suppose our mother went hungry; I suppose at the time we assumed she had a secret stash – she'd become so unpredictable we believed nothing she said.) That night I realized how alone we were, and I vowed that one day I'd take care of Billy.

Next morning he told me to stay home from school. We had corn flakes again for breakfast, the two of us sitting at the table like a regular family. Then Billy left the house, telling me not to leave until he came back. I waited by the window until I saw him turn the corner at two o'clock and ran outside to meet him.

"It came," I yelled, waving the money order.

I think he was disappointed. In the kitchen he took out two $10 bills and laid them on the table to show them to me.

"Where did you get it?"

Billy shook his head with an air that said he'd earned the right not to tell me. We ate our burgers that day like two friends who could take on the world together and win.

Fifteen years later I called him one day in Manhattan because I hadn't heard from him in almost three months. His phone was disconnected and Directory Assistance had no new listing for him. I realized I didn't have the name of a single friend or acquaintance of Billy's I could call to find out what had happened.

The next night I waited for four hours outside the warehouse building on Gansevoort Street, in the middle of the meat packing district. It was August, and even near the river the dead end-of-summer air seemed scarcely capable of supporting basic life. Nobody was answering bells in the warehouse building, probably because they were illegal occupants of industrial space. At midnight a couple who'd lived below Billy came home and told me they'd realized he'd left weeks ago when they stopped finding empty liquor bottles in the trash. They believed the woman he'd sublet from was still living in a yurt in the White Mountains, and they didn't have an address for her and certainly not a phone number.

The next night, drunk, I decided that Billy was probably dead. Because I couldn't stand doing nothing, I hired a private investigator to find out, the way I hired a private investigator later when our mother died to find out if our father was still alive. Billy called me at two o'clock one morning to borrow $500. Which was how I learned he'd moved to San Francisco. As I remember it, I felt infinitely lonelier when Billy called to borrow the money than when I realized I had to pay someone to find out if our last relative was still alive.

Chapter Eighteen

A SUNBURNT YOUNG man in rags sat on the sidewalk propped against the wall of the old bread factory.

"Do you know what I want?" he asked me.

Shannon Shepard and I disliked each other on sight. I think her dislike of me started it. When I first looked at her her eyes flicked away like Tom's when he caught me watching him. When she looked back her face had hardened and she was almost glaring with hostility.

There was nothing to dislike in her appearance. She was a pretty big-breasted woman with short blonde hair and a mouth that she kept too tight. I don't remember what her eyes were like because she kept averting them. I suppose she was in her early 30's. She wore jeans and an army surplus shirt with the sleeves rolled up. Later, when I saw her talking to other people, she was able to seem warm and competent and only a little harassed. I might have trusted her if I hadn't been able to enrage her without even trying.

"How can I help you?" Shannon asked with a certain amount of unconcealed hatred. I thought she was ridiculous, and I felt triumphant and sad.

"I'd like to hear about what you do here," I said.

Her mouth tightened further. "I led a guided tour for the Mayor's Office and the Health Department last week," she said. "I wish you'd been able to come then."

"So do I. I called you all last week and you didn't return my calls."

She glared at me, then looked away, hesitating, I guess over how badly she could afford to behave. I thought how hard it must be for her to get through a day with so much to be angry at, with so many surrogates to be punished for the unforgiven original outrages.

A young man on duty in the office at the top of the stairs had directed me to Shannon's office in the basement, behind the room where Marlin led the Sunday meeting and where two men were now setting up long tables. Her office was a cubicle barely big enough for a desk and two filing cabinets and two chairs, in a corner of a poorly lit corridor carpeted with the same shiny hard red carpet. I thought most of the sour-sweet smell would go if they took up the carpet, but they probably needed it to protect the floor, which felt unnervingly flimsy underfoot. There were two more locked cubicles further down the corridor, which ended in a laundry room with washers and driers. Shannon and I had to raise our voices to be heard over the noise from the kitchen. A few feet from where we sat four more men, looking tanned and fit in the jeans and brightly colored T-shirts that seemed to be uniform for the help at the Factory and the Dormitory, were washing and chopping vegetables and browning meat in two large pots on an institution-sized gas stove. They didn't lower their voices for our benefit and their chatter seemed trivial to me and their methods inefficient. But it was a long time since I'd been part of a team. I wasn't used to making allowances for other people's habits and needs.

"Is it hard to get volunteers?" I asked Shannon, indicating the kitchen workers and trying to lower the tension.

"Yes," she said, and stared at the workers in order not to look at me. "But those aren't volunteers. They're part of the staff."

"How many staff do you have?"

"Twelve," Shannon said. "I have two assistants, and Marlin has an assistant who also handles our finances, and we have two people to help us supervise the volunteers at night and six others to take care of everything else that's involved in running the Dormitory and raising money."

"I didn't realize it was such a big operation."

"We can house a hundred homeless PWA's a night," Shannon said. "So far we haven't had to turn anyone away."

"Men only?" I asked. Which provoked another tightening of

the mouth. I felt that I was dealing with ramifications of a discontent I could hardly begin to understand.

"At the moment," Shannon said. She shifted into automatic. "It would be different if this was New York, where the largest group of AIDS sufferers are IV drug users and a large percentage of them are homeless. We're still only seeing the beginnings of the AIDS drug users problem in San Francisco and so far we haven't seen any homeless women here. We've sent the word out, and I keep hearing rumors from the men that there are women out there on the streets, but they never materialize."

Shannon's expertise seemed to float free of her personal problems. I trusted what she said about the issues, give or take some occupational bias, and any need she might have to mislead me.

"Could you lead me through what happens when the men get here?" I asked.

"No problem," she sighed. "We open at six o'clock. We used to open at four, but it was more than the staff and volunteers could take. In any case a lot of the volunteers have paying jobs and they can't get here earlier. By six o'clock any agencies where the men might have business during the day are closed, though they tend to steer clear of other agencies. We hope that if they've spent the day on the streets they'll be grateful enough to give us as little trouble as possible."

"They don't have to be clean to get a bed at the Dormitory?"

Shannon laughed in my face. "If they had to be clean we'd go out of business. If they were clean and not likely to be disruptive they'd qualify for Shanti residences sharing independent housing with other AIDS patients. The men who come here not only have HIV disease. They're street drunks or IV drug users or both, and some have been in psychiatric hospitals, and they can't cope with the requirements of the city's other homeless programs. They're never clean long enough to go to an interview at the one or two substance abuse treatment programs that do take PWA's, and in any case they don't have health insurance, and they can't follow through on outpatient clinic treatment for their HIV diseases at General because they're too stoned. The ones who do end up as inpatients on the AIDS ward at General wander off in the middle of treatment or start trying to score off the other patients the minute they start to feel better."

"I admire you for doing the work," I said, sincerely. "How did you get involved? A heterosexual – I have to be careful in San Francisco, a presumably heterosexual –"

"Actually I'm bisexual, theoretically at least," Shannon said formally, as if she were reciting a script. I wondered why anyone would want to be bisexual these days. I thought how carefully and painfully she'd constructed herself and her theoretical positions, carefully building a house of cards.

"Mar and I go back a long way," she said with some irony. "He called me when he had an opening." She rushed on, getting businesslike again to show me I was a nuisance. "The line starts to form outside any time after lunchtime. Some of the men just crash in the courtyard until it's time to let them in. I do the initial assessment of each client or one of my assistants does it on the two evenings I'm not here. Ideally a client will be ambulatory and sufficiently together to give us his clothes and take a shower, in which case we'll give him clean clothes which are his to keep if his own clothes aren't worth washing. If he's too stoned or sick a volunteer will try to get him undressed and give him a bed wash and help him eat while the others are eating dinner downstairs."

"May I look at the rooms?" I asked.

"Come with me," she said. She locked her door behind her as if the inmates might want to take over the institution and led me to a staircase off the basement corridor. As we climbed I soon lost my sense of what floor we were on. Each floor seemed to have a dark TV room and well-lit toilets and washrooms. Every other square foot of space was taken up with narrow green corridors, lit by dim ceiling lights, and row after row of doorless cubicles, with more cubicles tucked around corners and up flights of stairs that stopped halfway between floors. Each cubicle had a thin mattress on a wooden bunk, a sheet, a pillow and a folded blanket, a hook for clothes and an unshaded bulb at head level. The cubicle was exactly twice as wide as the bunk. The air everywhere smelled of the same sickly smell mixed with ammonia. The empty shadows in the windowless rooms and corridors were hot and black. I imagined the Dormitory crowded at night with disease and pain and narcotic movement and my respect for Shannon increased.

Twice she quickly and firmly blocked me when I started to go down a dark corridor. "That's a dead end." "That's another dead end."

Maybe. But I knew I'd never be able to find these corners again to uncover what was really there.

"What happened to the doors?"

"The old owners took them off years ago to try to comply with the city's safe sex regulations. Business dropped off so badly at the bathhouses in the early 80's they had to close anyway. I'm sure Mar would put doors back on if we had the money. Homeless PWA's have as much right to privacy as anyone else."

"Have you set aside a special section for women in case they do show up?"

"Good question," Shannon said without conviction. She'd started leading me aimlessly up and down corridors while she examined details of walls and floors, barely discernible in the dark, for no reason other than to avoid meeting my eyes. "No, we haven't. I'll have to ask Mar what his policy would be on that. We don't prohibit the patients from visiting each other's rooms so I don't think it would make sense to isolate the women."

"Can the patients have sex?"

"If you mean do we allow them to have sex on the premises, officially no, but off the record we'd turn a blind eye. If you mean are they physically capable of having sex, probably not. They're ill, they're high or in withdrawal, they're physically and emotionally exhausted from the streets."

I let it go, but I doubted if what Shannon said was always true: I remembered the powerful sexual urgency that would overcome me in the middle of a near-blackout when I was otherwise hardly capable of moving.

Shannon surprised me. "They may occasionally indulge in a little halfhearted fellatio," she said. "Most of them have gone way beyond identifying themselves as either straight or gay. Choosing a sexual preference is the least of their troubles."

I led her into a TV room, which had three carpeted tiers to sit on while you watched an ancient RCA.

"The last owners had an up-to-date video system," Shannon said, "but they took it with them."

I sat down on the bottom tier. Shannon remained standing beside me as if she might end the interview at any moment. "How does the community feel about the kind of thing you've just told me? Some anti-gay groups could have a field day accusing you of helping to spread AIDS by letting patients have sex."

She hesitated over her response. "How do *you* feel about it?"

"I admire all of you for what you're doing. I'm just surprised that some people let you get away with it. I can imagine a headline in the *National Enquirer*: 'Sex Orgies in San Francisco AIDS Hospital.' Or some ultraconservative group using you as proof that degenerates will have sex under any circumstances."

Shannon nodded. "The conservatives don't risk getting close enough to see what's really going on. They're too busy making money demanding forced testing and quarantines and scaring their congregations into coughing up money. The media and the Health Department are sympathetic. They don't ask the kind of dumb questions that could get us into trouble. Of course homeless PWA's sometimes have sex. But if they have it with each other at the Dormitory they're containing the disease, not spreading it to others who are uninfected. If federal prisons can't stop prisoners having sex we surely can't. Mar says our mission is to let the clients do as they wish, as far as we possibly can. But we don't allow drugs. We could be closed down if they found drugs here."

I looked up and stared at Shannon until she was forced to meet my gaze in the half-light from the corridor.

"Did you know my brother Billy?" I asked.

She looked relieved. "No," she said quickly, and turned to examine the blank TV screen. "I don't even remember him from the transfer. But I don't always go. We do it so often now because we need so many volunteers and there's such a high turnover."

"Who would know Billy? Someone must know him well if he worked here."

"The woman who was in charge of volunteers. He left six months ago, you know."

"Can I talk to her?"

"She doesn't work for us any more. She took a job with the city as an AIDS educator."

"What's her name?"

"I'll ask her to get in touch with you," Shannon said. "It's not fair for her to keep getting calls at work about Dormitory business."

Everything Shannon had said about Billy sounded glib and overprepared to me.

"How did you know when Billy stopped working here?" I asked.

"I checked his folder when I knew you were coming," she said unwillingly.

"Can I see it?"

"No. It contains very personal information and confidential evaluations by Dormitory staff. There's no reason in it why Billy left. He just stopped showing up. Valerie –" (she checked herself too late) "– wrote a note saying she'd tried to contact him but he didn't return her calls."

"If the police were to get a search warrant you'd have to show them the folder."

"I'm not so sure about that," Shannon said, her voice rising. "The folder probably counts as privileged information, like a therapist's records."

"A therapist's records? What can you mean? You're not professionals."

That stung her. "We regard ourselves as very professional," Shannon snapped. "We have a duty to the city to keep our records confidential. Our clients and the volunteers need to know that the information they give us will be kept confidential."

"Okay," I said, trying to slow it down. "Do you understand why I'd like to see the folder? I want to find out as much as possible about Billy in the last year of his life."

The appeal didn't work. She was spinning out of control, I thought far beyond any provocation by me, and she was enjoying herself. "We don't create records on our volunteers so that they can be plundered by family members with guilty consciences," she snapped.

I waited a little to let both of us feel the effects of what she'd said. "Let's go down to your office," I said, and led the way to a flight of stairs near the washroom area without turning to see if she followed. I was glad to get out of the TV room. As my eyes grew accustomed to the dark I'd begun to notice that the carpet I was sitting on had stains I preferred not to speculate about.

I hurried downstairs, elated. Shannon could have provoked easy anger in me if I wasn't so accustomed to swallowing my own random anger in the interests of keeping sober. But it was hard to take her rage personally, because she was too transparently troubled. I remembered a rule I'd learned in meetings: If a speaker gets angry or tries to provoke anger in you, they're sicker than you are. I'd barely felt present talking to Shannon in those strange dark rooms where the air was charged with shadows of sex and disease – she was too busy trying to take revenge on other men I'd never know anything about. I'd been watching myself take my own deliberate revenge by withdrawing from her emotionally, as if she wasn't worth the trouble. I felt the way I used to when a deposition witness lost control and started revealing more than he needed to.

One floor down I entered three dead-end corridors before I found the staircase that led down to the reception area. From there I took the long route to Shannon's basement office because I knew the way. The large room where two long dining tables had now been set up had the empty air of a theater or conference hall after the illusionists or pitchmen have gone. I even missed the cheap excitement of candles and incense and music.

When I turned into the corridor of offices Shannon was nowhere in sight, but the doors of the other two offices were open. Marlin's blond bodyguard was sitting in the cubicle next to Shannon's, laboriously entering a column of figures on a calculator. I knocked and introduced myself. He grinned at me, happy and friendly and overwhelmed.

I indicated the calculator. "I saw you here the Sunday before last. I thought you were Marlin's bodyguard."

"Sort of," he said. "I'm his lover. And I handle the money." He put down the calculator to talk to me, poked at a key, maybe to record a subtotal, and checked the display.

"Whoops!" he said, then shrugged and grinned. "I lost it." He was an impressive sight that didn't stand up to close inspection. His pectorals and biceps were huge balls of muscle, but the rest of his upper body didn't seem to have been worked on proportionately; the thin wrists and love handles made him look vulnerable after all, and there were deep folds of skin at his armpits and neck. I realized that he was closer to 40 than 25, and that his boyish-looking hair was dyed. He wore a yellow muscle shirt that barely covered his sternum. His exposed nipples, which looked enlarged and leathery, each supported a small gold ring.

"I'm glad I ran into you," I said. "I was going to ask Shannon for a balance sheet."

"We do one of those," he said cheerfully. "We just sent one out in our newsletter." He hunted around and gave me a stapled photocopied handout with the Dormitory's logo – a crudely drawn flame inside a circle – at the top of the first page.

"What's that?" Shannon asked at my elbow, glaring at Mar's lover.

"There you are," I said. "We were just introducing ourselves." I folded the handout without letting her see what it was, to enrage her a little further, and put it in my back pocket as I moved back to her office and waited for her to open the door. She hesitated before following me, searching the kitchen for an escape before she finally unlocked it.

"How much longer is this going to take?" she asked.

"About 20 minutes. He didn't tell me his name."

"Wink," she said, the mouth tightening again.

"I'm curious," I said evenly. "What makes you think you can get away with being ill-mannered and impatient and consumed with anger when I come along with an offer of money for the Dormitory? Is the city so generous with its money that you already have everything you need for the clients?"

Her look of relief, of tension released, included surprise. "Mar said nothing about money," she said. "He told me you were trying to find out what happened to your brother."

So Mar hadn't even paid lip service to my excuse for coming to the Dormitory.

"My brother was murdered," I said. "You save all your compassion for men who have AIDS?"

"I've told you I don't know anything about your brother," Shannon said, her voice rising. "Our job here is hard enough. We don't have time for all this extra trouble."

"Billy isn't extra. He volunteered here. If it wasn't for men like him supporting your work you wouldn't have a job."

Shannon laughed. "We're paid a pittance for what we go through here."

"I'm sure there are other jobs."

"Don't tell –"

"Your remark about guilty families was deeply offensive and irresponsible. Now I have a few more questions I want you to answer. If you choose not to, I'll take my questions to the police and the Health Department."

Shannon shrugged, her face scarlet, her body trembling. "I believe any two people can settle their differences if they both try," she managed. I think she meant it. I felt sleazy.

"What exactly do the volunteers do with the clients? What would Billy have done?"

She tried to turn down the anger by switching to automatic again. "Each client is assigned to a volunteer after I've finished the assessment interview. Mainly I try to decide if the clients are capable of being hooked up with any of the other services that are available. If I think they are, one of my assistants tries to take care of the liaison work the next morning."

"But what exactly do the *volunteers* do?"

"We teach them how to be *with* the client, to listen, to comfort them physically if they're detoxing, to massage them to relieve pain and help them sleep. We also teach the volunteers how to defend themselves nonviolently. I think everyone who works here is a pacifist, but we need to protect ourselves. We try to weed out – to prevent obviously threatening clients from getting into the Dormitory, but they can be threatening by their very nature, and of course their behavior fluctuates. It isn't always possible to tell ahead of time how they'll behave."

"And all this training goes on at what you call the transfer?"

She nodded, her eyes starting to clear as she demonstrated her expertise. "Volunteers are here for 36 hours uninterrupted training."

"Why is it called the transfer?"

"Mar transfers all his ideas and all that he's learned about dealing with homeless PWA's."

"Why does it take 36 hours?"

"We train the volunteers to put themselves into the client's life space. The first night they're here we encourage them to imagine that they're dying of AIDS alone on the streets of San Francisco, which is exactly what would happen to most of the clients if the Dormitory didn't exist. We pretend this whole basement area is a parking lot South of Market on a winter night. The volunteers role-play clients who are hungry and weak and in foul clothes and looking for someplace to sleep, and we show them what might happen to them on any night. They keep being moved on by police, and then angry residents and other street people start assaulting them."

"You act all that out?"

"Experiential psychodrama works far better than any theoretical training. Staff and volunteers who've already been through the training act the parts of the authorities."

"Let me guess," I said. "I bet the volunteers aren't allowed to sleep the first night."

"Right," Shannon said with enthusiasm, "or if they do manage to drift off we wake them up. Most of them are so shattered by the experience that they can't sleep the next day either. Mar found that the best way to teach them to empathize with the clients was to put them directly in touch with their own pain and fears of abandonment. Our volunteers want to feel empowered by doing something to fight their feelings of helplessness in the epidemic. I think the transfer makes them realize how close to the edge they are themselves – all it would need is a city that decided to stop spending sufficient money on AIDS care, or a city that's finally overwhelmed by the numbers of AIDS patients. You don't even have to have AIDS to be homeless these days."

Shannon's anger had been replaced by zeal. I realized she had no notion that what the Dormitory did was manipulative and intrusive. I imagined Billy being abused by these people and felt the birth of cold hatred for them. It cooled me like reason, and made me feel calmly in charge of what I did.

"We make it up to them," Shannon said, sounding to me like a heartless fool. "We assign someone to each new volunteer for the rest of the transfer and we really nurture them and guide them through everything they're feeling. That's how they open themselves to what it feels like to the clients to have the Dormitory to come to."

"So you make the volunteers emotionally vulnerable," I said, "and very dependent on you for support. And you show them how important the work is. That must make them feel guilty if they want to criticize what you do or if they decide to leave."

She nodded along as she listened to me, seemingly not noticing my disapproval. "It doesn't always work. We require a three-month commitment, but some of the volunteers don't last that long. And some people aren't suited to the work at all."

"You mean you turn down people?"

"Oh yes. We assess everyone during the transfer and we tell them if we don't feel they're suitable."

"What kind of volunteer would be unsuitable?"

"Some people can't handle the feelings that arise. Some people get very angry during the transfer."

"I wonder why," I said. "Do you tell them in advance what they can expect to go through?"

"They know it's going to be experiential," she said. "We try to keep the details confidential so that volunteers can experience it all as fully as possible. We find that hardly any of our workers talk about it outside the Dormitory. Everyone who's been through it seems to want to guard it for the others."

"What were you doing before you started working here?"

"I was a psychotherapist with my own private practice," Shannon said rather grandly.

"That must be a great help in the work here. What are you? A psychologist? A clinical social worker?"

Her mouth tightened and hardened, as I'd guessed it would. "I was a therapist. I specialized in an interactive phenomenological approach."

"But what kind of license did you have?"

Her mouth tightened so hard that she made a sucking noise as she glared at me. No license.

"Billy's apartment was searched, presumably by whoever murdered him. Do you have any idea what they might have been looking for?"

She shifted immediately into blank innocence.

Then two things happened almost simultaneously. Steam billowed into the end of the corridor as a door opened. A tall naked black man emerged from the steam, which snipped off when the door closed behind him. He stood toweling himself in full view of all of us, his cock and balls swinging. And Mar stepped into the corridor from the side staircase, the lower half of his body almost hidden by the maroon Macy's shopping bag he carried. He wore a smaller size of the same yellow tank top that Wink was wearing, but it hung loosely on his white and narrow chest. He began to turn towards us but his attention was attracted by the tall black.

Mar set down his shopping bag and crossed over to the naked

man. He reached up, put his hands on the man's ears and pulled down his head, pushing his body into the other man's body. He kissed him on the mouth. I saw that the man's arms and shoulders were covered with lesions blacker than his skin. Mar placed his hands on the man's chest and whispered something in his ear. The man nodded. As Mar turned away his hand drifted down the man's body.

Mar retrieved his shopping bag and set it outside the door of the empty office, kissed his lover – who looked affectionate and unjealous – on the mouth, and walked over to Shannon and me. The front of his trousers was wet. He glanced shrewdly at Shannon, I think checking her emotional condition, then turned and looked up at me.

"You've been to the hairdresser," Mar said. "You look radiant."

Chapter Nineteen

WHEN I REACHED the top of the stairs that led down to the street, the man in the glass-walled office was sorting clothes with his back to me. I moved to walk past him down the stairs, then I stepped back, then I moved to the right and stopped. There was another office counter inside the front door, presumably so that he could talk to clients who'd already been admitted or were about to leave. The man in the office, who was lean and short and bald, and older than the usual Dormitory workers, all of which added up to my thinking of him as angry, still had his back to me. I glanced to the left – an empty red-carpeted corridor with the beginnings or endings of various flights of stairs. To the right the full-length mirror flanked by stairs. This time I stared at myself, wondering what I was going to do: I looked open-mouthed, at a loss, gawky. Not at all what I expected to look like.

The man a few feet away finished sorting a pile of threadbare cotton shirts. His hand rested on them as he paused and prepared himself for what he'd do next. He was about to turn. I moved to the right against the mirror to prevent him seeing me, then I stepped up two stairs in case he'd heard me and came into the corridor. Then I had nowhere to go except upstairs, leaping urgently as if the hounds of hell were after me. One of the stairs creaked as I landed on it. I froze, then moved to the side and began to climb cautiously, testing with the heels of my loafers. Then I grew even more nervous when I realized that anyone who saw the way I moved would know I didn't belong in the Dormitory. My clothes brushing against the wetness when I moved made me realize I was already covered in sweat. All the training I'd submitted to told me I was doing the wrong thing. However squalid my private life, my public behavior had usually been impeccable, at least when I was sober.

I'd moved almost before I realized why: I was going to steal Billy's file from Shannon Shepard's office. Which meant I'd have to hide until the middle of the night, when I hoped clients and staff would be asleep. I was climbing the stairs to find a corner to hide in until then. On the tour with Shannon I thought I'd counted two full floors above the reception area and what looked like a truncated top floor, as if they'd jerry-built partitions in an attic to satisfy the need for rooms where men tried to satisfy insatiable needs. I felt comfortable with the ghosts in this building. I knew how the need to fuck became imperative when I'd been drinking, how irritable and unsatisfied I felt the moment the need was met, how the need immediately started rekindling.

I knew the main floors were connected by at least two sets of staircases at opposite ends of the building, but I'd noticed that the location of the stairs changed between different floors, and that everything else also seemed to change location: the washrooms, the TV rooms, the dead-end staircases crammed between floors. The building was a labyrinth.

The narrow stairway I was climbing was lit only by light leaking from the reception area below, which meant that it turned before it reached the next floor. I had no idea what it led to - the steeper shorter staircase I'd used to get away from Shannon had been on the other side of the hall. I slowed as I approached the dark turn, then edged up and saw that the stairway continued above me to the left, twisting around some core function of the building. There was still darkness at the top, and now the stairs were pitch black. I half laughed at myself, recognizing the inevitable, that I would always manage to get myself to where I didn't want to go. Even as an adult I was still occasionally surprised by fear of the dark, of the grinning murderer at the top of the stairs, the shape waiting to clutch me as I stepped into the dark hall. When I was 20 years younger and more ashamed of who I was, I forced myself to tell my wife about those fears. We'd gone out to dinner on one of the occasions when we'd both been able to agree to discuss our differences. As a sign of my determination to show vulnerability,

I came up with the dread I'd sometimes discover in myself when I was alone in a hotel room or in the New York apartment. Never a warning that the fear was coming. My wife looked sorry for me and I started to get angry. "You're very lonely," she said. I shut down: What was the good of talking if she started making unsupported diagnoses that fitted her own agenda?

I was still sweating, and I started to fear that I'd panic. I waited, feeling my breath get heavier. But the terror didn't come. I began trying to convince myself that I welcomed this darkness. It felt safe because it was familiar. The reddish black air bore the familiar smells and temperatures of other makeshift pleasure palaces I'd once been at home in.

It was light I had to fear, and when I emerged on the third floor there was the light of a washroom next to a wider staircase to my left. The usual dark cubicles were lined up across the corridor and to either side of me. Still no sign or sound of anyone else this high up in the building at this time of the afternoon. It was about five o'clock, so the clients would still be lining up to get in. I peered down the corridor to the left, searching for a continuation of the staircase I'd just climbed. It was light enough to see the pillows at the back of the bunks in the cubicles, but I could see no sign of another upward staircase.

I moved to the right, away from the light, checking over my shoulder as I edged along from cubicle to cubicle, ready to melt inside if I saw or heard anyone. I was backing into deeper darkness, and I nearly bumped into the wall at the end of the corridor before I saw it. I moved into the empty space to my right. I could dimly make out the different intensities of darkness outlining the cubicle doorways on both sides as I moved along with outstretched arms. Three, four, on each side. Then a wall in front of me. I was beginning to feel completely safe in this dark world I had to myself. I moved back across the main corridor. Another corridor, again with cubicles on both sides. This time the doorways ended but I was still able to walk forward. The tips of my fingers outlined an archway. Dense blackness inside. Maybe this was what Shannon had been hiding from me. The entrance was as hard to resist as all the parts of town that had beckoned when I was younger, where it had to be happening, the places I never seemed to be.

Six feet inside the archway there was a long wooden wall. I

hugged the wall and followed it towards the side of the archway until I touched a plaster wall in front of me. To the right I felt a space about a foot wide, and I turned into it. Still no light. The faint sounds from the rest of the building that had been echoing in the corridors outside cut off completely. I held onto the edge of the long wall and moved into the darkness as far as I could. I knew enough not to let go of the wall until I knew exactly where it was behind me. I reached out and felt other walls in front of me and on either side, other edges. The moment I began to fear I was in a maze I took one step back to safety, past the edge of the wall where I'd entered, and turned left back into the area in front of the archway. But now there were close black walls on all sides of me and only one space, to my left where there shouldn't be space. I was already deep in the maze.

I was angry at myself for being so stupid, but I was also surprised to feel relief. The trap, if it was a trap for intruders, was also an escape. I had eight or nine hours, until three or four in the morning, to find my way out. In the meantime, as long as I was inside the maze, no one was likely to discover me. I was also angry because of course it was an outrage that this area, presumably built for perfectly anonymous sucking and fucking, and a potential death trap for any stoned or demented client who wandered into it, should not have been boarded up when Mar converted the bathhouse into the Dormitory. I wondered how anyone could trust Mar with people's lives or even take him seriously.

I counted to ten, took a few deep breaths, then slowly lowered my butt, careful never to touch the floor with my hands. At least the carpet I sat on felt dry. Schoolboy adventure solutions were running through my head. I thought of tearing my shirt into thin strips and making a rope so that I'd know when I doubled back on my path through the maze. But I needed to find something to tie the end to. Maybe I could make a hole in one of the wooden partitions and hook the cloth around a splinter. I remembered drafts, another solution from adventure stories, and waited to feel the draft that would lead me to the entrance. The air was still. I was sure I'd see more when my eyes grew accustomed to the blackness. It occurred to me that in the bathhouse days the maze couldn't possibly have been pitch black because of the risk of men already high on drugs or alcohol creating panic. There must be a ceiling light somewhere. Except that the switch was probably controlled from the office. The darkness refused to become more penetrable.

My head jerked as if I'd caught myself napping. I was exhausted from the nastiness with Shannon and the tension of the flight into the upper building. I noticed that the sweat on the front of my shirt had dried. I tried checking my watch to see if I'd really slept, but the lighting on the digital display worked no better than ever. I got an indecipherable sidelit display. Finally it occurred to me to use the enemy's tactics. I needed to relax, so I closed my eyes and tried to visualize Mar's flame guiding me out of the maze. I stretched out my legs closer to the floor so that I could breathe more deeply.

The red candle melted and dropped away and I saw only the white and yellow flame at the end of a long hall where doors kept opening for the flame as I followed it and the walls rushed past me. Then Billy's Greenwich Village vampire came flying out of a doorway and soared down the hall to smother me.

I knew I'd been sleeping because I knew exactly where the vampire in the dream had come from. Billy and I had once compared acid experiences – I could count mine on the fingers of one hand and wanted to know what I'd missed. Billy told me about the man he'd picked up on Christopher and gone home with to a small apartment on Bank Street, two rooms off a hallway. Dropping the acid had been involuntary that time – his trick slipped it to him in a drink. Billy came to as the trick darted a plastic lizard in his face. Then the man went away and came back the next second in slow motion down the endless little hallway in a vampire cape and vampire fangs. Billy found himself pressing the point of a dagger against the vampire's throat. He knew it was okay to push the dagger into the flesh because this was only an acid game. "That's enough," the trick said, rescuing himself, on that occasion at least.

I once dropped mescalin in the presence of a whore who declined her share. I told her to work on my dick and she did it the way I liked, for what felt like a long time, maybe hours. "Oh yeah, oh yeah," I said as she took care of me, almost embarrassed as she got so close to the core. "Yeah, yeah," I moaned as I let her learn what I was about. I was full of impersonal gratitude.

In a moment's shift I knew that I was fully awake and hearing the same grateful sound here in the maze, a wooden wall or two away from me. "Oh yes," someone moaned. "Oh yes." A grunt. Silence. I waited, ready to crawl in the direction of the next sound I heard, no matter what residues I disturbed on the floor. There was a skitter or a patter and I froze, bewildered by the sound, fearing it might be a rat. The sound quickly increased in frequency and volume to a regular drumming, still unrecognizable. Then a beating, then a banging on a wall to my left, the impact so hard that I imagined displaced air pushing towards me. Then a few inches away I heard a short broken squawk like one of the seabirds at Ocean Beach. It had to be a human cry, but I knew of no plausible circumstances under which a human being would utter such a cry. The banging continued even louder, but now it was on another wall farther away. The seabird squawked. Pause. Squawk. The banging got louder, became breaking thuds, but still regular, mechanical. Then there was a tearing splintering sound and a tentative mist of brown light wandered a few inches around the end of a wall in front of me and seemed to stop right there. It was enough to rob the maze of any terror – the first thing I noticed was that even the ubiquitous red carpet looked relatively clean – and show me how small the maze really was. The long wall a few black-painted boards away on my right must be the wall in front of the archway I'd entered through, and it was about eight feet away, beyond boards nailed together at right angles and reaching only six inches above my head when I stood up.

I heard rhythmic sounds again, a drumming or a chatter, both. Then a short howling yelp, and another, and then others repeated at regular but longer intervals than the drumming and chatter. What might have occurred to me then didn't occur until I told Luke about it afterwards, that Mar or his helpers were staging a performance to draw me out of the maze. I think it felt too raw not to be real.

As I edged round the wall where the light stole in the drumming and the chatter and the howling yelp grew louder. The exit from the maze lay two flimsy wooden partitions away; I glimpsed human but otherwise unidentifiable movement close to a splintered hole in the last partition. I peered around its edge, not knowing what to expect, and came face to face with Mar as if he had been waiting for me, standing staring in my direction inside an archway identical to the one where I'd entered the maze, though I noted that this archway must be at another end because directly behind Mar there was a brightly lit washroom. Mar opened his mouth and yelped, then shut his mouth. He was naked, his small white penis erect, as out of control as the rest of him. I almost took flight, but it was abundantly clear from the scene before me that I was the last thing on anyone else's mind.

The drumming and the chatter came from the tall black Mar had fondled outside the shower room. He was bouncing back and forth against the black wooden partition inside the archway as if attached to it by hundreds of short strong rubber bands. He was still naked, or naked again, his genitals bouncing with the rest of him. The chattering was the sound of his teeth galloping out of control as if they'd jump out of his mouth. Mar yelped again. When I turned back to him I saw him staring through me, his eyes glassy. I doubted he was certain I was really there, he'd been rendered so abject by whatever chemicals he'd absorbed. Then the black man's drumming became unbearably fast, turning into one continuous sound, and his eyes started to roll back in his head. At the same time I heard shouts and footsteps coming up a staircase. I dashed over and cradled the back of the man's head in my hand and tried to tip it forwards. He resisted. The moment his skull got used to my hand it started to bounce back against my palm, forcing itself in the opposite direction to the way I wanted his head to go. His skin next to my hands looked as if it had been dusted with putty and was pocked and scarred as well as blotched with the dense black lesions. I grabbed his skull harder and pulled out my handkerchief and tried to make a funnel with it inside my free hand. Then I pried the man's teeth open with my middle finger and forced my fingers over his tongue and stuffed the handkerchief on top of it. Mar yelped beside me. The black man fell back against the wall, his shaking a little slowed. The voices sounded about to emerge onto the main staircase at the end of the corridor.

I darted back towards the maze, realized that the Dormitory people could trap me there by blocking the exits, and ran back into the corridor and into a cubicle next to Mar just as I saw Shannon's head emerge on the staircase. The cubicle wasn't dark enough to hide me. I tried huddling up in the corner of the cot next to the empty doorway but my feet on the edge of the cot showed in the brown light from the corridor. I slipped a pillow over my feet just as Shannon and two men, one of them Wink, ran past me towards Mar and the black man four or five feet away on the other side of the wooden wall. I thought: The handkerchief is hanging half out of his mouth. Who'll wonder first who put it there?

Shannon lost no time assessing the situation. "Take Edwin into a room," she instructed. *Not this one*. "We'll take Mar downstairs." Even as I waited to see if they were going to find me, I wondered at their priorities: Shannon and Wink to tend to a stoned Mar, one worker to nurse a client in the middle of a drug- or disease-induced seizure. They did wait while the young man in a blue T-shirt led Edwin into a cubicle on the other side of the hall, just beyond the narrow slice of corridor I could see through the doorway without poking my head too far out into the shadowed corner. Shannon and Mar and Wink were still behind the wall to my left, but they started moving past my cubicle, Shannon and Wink on each side of a compliant, still naked Mar, thick folds of skin hanging under his small loose buttocks. I was safe.

Then Mar whirled and pointed through the doorway of my cubicle. He yelped. We stared in each other's direction but I was sure I must be the only one of us who could see. His eyes still looked glazed, though less helpless, in the shadowy brown corridor light. I prayed that it was surely impossible for Wink or Shannon to see into my corner from where they were standing.

Wink reached up to take his lover's hand. "I'm going to take you home," he said.

Mar pulled his hand away and pointed at me again.

"Come on, Mar," Shannon said impatiently. "We need to get some clothes on you before the volunteers see you."

Mar's eyes, possibly his memory, emptied as they spun him around and led him away. The sound of their footsteps finally died in the stairwell. Now that I was safe again my heart started to pound and fear flowed through my gut like a black dye. Along with it I felt a kind of boyish glee. All this might be deadly serious, but it was also closer to kid's adventure stories than anything else that had ever happened to me. Billy and I had grown up far too soon.

A crooning started in the cubicle where the volunteer had

taken Edwin. I thought I'd better move; maybe Shannon or Wink would finally start to wonder how the handkerchief got in Edwin's mouth, or decide it might be as well to investigate what Mar had been pointing at. I thought it should be safe to go back through the maze now, but I'd glimpsed a recess on this side of the corridor that might be another upward staircase, and I wanted to investigate alternative exits in case I needed to make a quick getaway later in the night. Taking that route meant I'd have to pass Edwin and his worker, but I was prepared to risk being seen. I wanted to see how Edwin was doing, and I hoped I could pass for a volunteer if anyone but Mar and his cronies caught sight of me.

I paused in the shadows outside Edwin's cubicle, trying to be quiet enough not to be noticed, but trying not to look furtive in case I was seen. The light was on, softened by a pillowcase draped over the bulb. Edwin lay full-length on the cot with his head propped against a pillow. The man in the blue T-shirt sat beside him with his back to me, holding Edwin's hand.

"The flame flows through your body," he crooned, "pushing pain away like foam. The flame fills your body with light."

Edwin caught sight of me. "Thank you partner," he said.

I nodded and winked.

"That's all right," the man in the blue T-shirt said. "That's what I'm here for."

The staircase brought me to another corridor on the fourth floor. The same brown light. No signs of life. I started to move less cautiously. I could see no sign of fire exits or ladders, but I found a short staircase in a truncated corner of the building that I'd passed earlier in the day. I pushed open the metal bar of the door at the top and met a neon sky and air so hot it felt like exhaust from the noisy trucks below. When I found myself basking in the air because it was so dry, I realized how humid the cubicles and corridors inside the Dormitory were.

I was standing on the edge of a small rooftop area carpeted with green plastic turf. The area had been swept clean and there was nothing among the air vents and closed off chimneys, not a brick or plank, to prop the door open behind me. I used one of my loafers. Most of the traffic noise came from the left, where only a six inch upright metal strip prevented anyone walking off the roof and hitting the steady industrial stream in the wide street below. Back across the roof – which was presumably where bathhouse patrons had sunned themselves – opposite another metal curb, there were the gabled rooftops of a row of wooden houses; between the rooftop and the houses, a wide pit of an alley lit only by one or two lights in back rooms. The third side of the roof ended in the high blind blackened brick wall of the bread factory. No windows, no footholds. I left the only possible escape route to last: another brick wall that looked only inches higher than me. I reached up for the top of the wall. It was higher than it had looked. But there was plenty of running space in front of the wall. I kicked off the other loafer, took a running leap and landed halfway up the wall with a good grip on the top. Also a stubbed toe and a scraped hand. I heaved one foot onto the top of the wall, pulled my upper body after it, and found myself toppling forward, about to pitch into the blackness beneath. I kicked with the foot that was still beneath me and let myself fall backwards onto the rooftop. My shoulders and elbows took most of the impact of the hard surface under the plastic grass. I lay sickened for minutes before I got up, already stiff, and forced myself to lift my body up the wall again, more cautiously.

The roof of the body shop next door was about twelve feet below me, across a dark hole six or seven feet wide. I assumed there was dead space between the buildings, though I couldn't see what was at the bottom. One edge of the tarred rooftop below had the top of a white metal ladder hooked over it. I figured the top of the wall was wide enough to stand on, at least long enough to steady myself. I thought I could make the jump if I ever had to. But if I lost my footing or my balance I stood a good chance of falling into the hole and killing myself. I wasn't sure which prospect I preferred: to jump without full knowledge of what I was doing, or to jump in daylight, the vertigo worsened by seeing exactly where I might fall.

Chapter Twenty

OF COURSE I COULDN'T wait until three in the morning. It was nearer midnight when I left my cubicle and crept downstairs. The night had been strangely quiet. Wherever the AIDS homeless were sleeping this hot night it wasn't on the top floor of the Dormitory. Once or twice I'd heard the echo of an echo of a hard impact – a table being folded, a heavy door banged – but no other sound or sign of life. The Dormitory might have been closed down for the night.

I paused, listening, before I stepped off the stairs into the third floor corridor. The cubicles opposite me were empty, but now the air was filled with human presence. As soon as I poked my head into the corridor I felt the weight of coughs, moans, shadows, messages sent off by the bulk of bodies filling space, the hum of pain and desire. I edged out into the corridor, then slid quickly back against the wall. A man in a pink T-shirt stood in a doorway down the corridor, his back facing out. I could hear only the murmur of his talk. I needed to get past him and through the maze, to the stairs to the basement that bypassed the big room where I'd first seen Mar.

I decided to bluff it. I moved a couple of inches away from the wall and began to walk down the corridor as if I belonged there. As I approached the man his back remained turned away. I almost drew level. Then a hand reached out of a cubicle on my left and gripped my arm.

"I need to talk to you."

I jumped and whirled and had taken in the man who was

holding onto me before I had time to acknowledge fear. He was kneeling on the edge of the cot next to the doorway.

He stared at me and I stared back. I figured the best tactic was to keep my mouth shut as long as possible.

"I was lonely," he said finally, big-eyed and hollow-cheeked and distraught, with pale hair sticking out from his head like straw. He looked 25 years younger than me.

"Yeah," I said, easing out of the corridor and sitting down on the cot as if it was the natural thing for me to do. His body didn't look as if there was enough strength in the muscles to grip me that hard.

"Where is everyone tonight?" I asked, though I doubted he was in shape to volunteer accurate information.

He stared at me. I waited. "I've forgotten your name," I said.

"Joe," he said.

I scrambled for a name. "I'm Dave," I said.

"It's cold tonight," he said, and I started to search his face for more specific signs of sickness. I found only a look I recognized: a determination to play for time in the face of disaster. I looked down at his arms, which were three-quarters bare in the blue medic's shirt he wore. The inner arms were rutted where the veins should be and crowded with crusty sores.

I unfolded the blanket and draped it around Joe's shoulders. His bones felt brittle as burnt paper. "I'd be all right if my roommates would take me back," he said. "I think I'll go see them tomorrow. Come with me. You could make them understand we could get on all right."

"Where do they live?" I asked, playing for time.

"I think they moved," he said.

A shadow leapt along the corridor. The man in the pink T-shirt stood in the doorway, blocking it; all I could see was a black moustache and the suggestion of a chin.

"Hi," I said, smiling a fairly bright smile. "Joe wants us to find his roommates."

"Joe was assigned to me," he said coldly.

"Yeah. I saw you were busy." I gripped Joe's fragile shoulder for a moment. "Take care." And stood up. "He's all yours," I told the man as I pushed past. He stared or glared at me.

I walked down the corridor and turned right towards the maze, quickened by a conviction that my time was running out.

The maze was as I'd left it four hours ago. The light coming through the hole, which hadn't been trimmed or patched, made it easily negotiable. Both entrances were unguarded. The cubicles in the corridor at the other end were also heavy with human presences, but there were no signs of Dormitory workers. I passed along quickly and went down the stairs that had brought me to the upper part of the building earlier that night. As I approached the second floor I edged along the wall opposite the full-length mirror until I could see the reception area behind me. No one in sight. I darted past the mirror to the stairs opposite, which I guessed were the stairs I'd seen Mar come down with his Macy's shopping bag.

The laundry room was at the bottom to my left, the kitchen to my right. Both were closed down for the night. I walked quickly across to Shannon's office and tried the door. Locked, as I'd known it would be. It looked fragile enough to kick open but I figured the glass panel next to it would be quicker and quieter. I hit the corner next to the door hard with the heel of my hand. Nothing gave. I looked around for a cloth to tie around my shoe to muffle a blow, then I remembered seeing piles of colored T-shirts on top of the driers in the laundry room. I took off my shirt, tied it around my right loafer, then limped to the laundry room and found two large T-shirts and put on the red one on top of the blue one in case I needed a quick change of identity.

I couldn't believe how hard it was to kick in glass only a couple of inches above my waist. When it eventually broke I thought the crack and the ringing falling sounds would be heard all over the building. I knocked away enough glass to open the door from the inside, then closed it behind me.

There was a heavy pair of scissors on Shannon's desk that would have made short work of the filing cabinet locks, but it wasn't necessary to use them. The top drawer of the right-hand filing cabinet was unlocked and half-filled with folders. I could just see the typed names on the labels if I bent them towards the light from the corridor. Nothing for William Phillips, at least not in alphabetical order. The bottom drawer was empty. I moved to the left-hand cabinet. Also unlocked, and jammed tight with folders. Maybe these were the files for volunteers who no longer worked at the Dormitory. The name on the last folder in the top drawer was Henry Murray. I closed the drawer and opened the drawer below it. Billy's folder was about 20 folders in from the front. When I pulled it out it felt thinner than the others looked. I pulled out the folders around it to check – they felt much thicker. I hesitated. I thought that if I ever found myself having to explain what I'd done I could justify taking Billy's folder, but not anyone else's. I stuffed the other folders back in the drawer and closed it.

As I stepped out of the office the man in the pink T- shirt stepped off a staircase into the corridor to my left.

"Hi," I said. I waved to him with my shirt, walked quickly to the stairs opposite, then tore up to the lobby and ran up to the man at the reception desk, startling him at his paperback.

"There's an intruder," I yelled as I opened the front door. "They need you downstairs." I moved out onto the stairs. "I'm going for the police."

I tore down the stairs expecting someone to jump on my shoulders at any moment. Maybe I only imagined hearing my name called behind me as I passed through the door into the courtyard and ran for the street.

Chapter Twenty One

I GLANCED THROUGH Billy's folder in the taxi on the way home. All it contained was an essay Billy had written as part of his application to work at the Dormitory, and an evaluation scale that made my blood boil when I read it. Shannon had mentioned a notation by her predecessor about trying to reach Billy after he left, but even that was missing.

I didn't read Billy's essay until after I woke up near noon the next day, with the sun so hot it had already outlined a crumpled sweat man on the sheet beneath me. The application form was word processed with two different kinds of typeface and laser printed. Billy's essay had been badly typed on a machine whose correcting tape removed only the bottom half of the letters he tried to erase.

Tell us why you are interested in working at the Dormitory. What strengths and weaknesses do you bring with you? In what ways would you like to improve your personal growth?

I laughed out loud at the idea of Mar and Shannon improving Billy's personal growth. Then I read Billy's often incoherent response, a time capsule from a voice that had died.

I want this work so badly. These times are terrible. We are being attacked from outside us and inside ourselves by virus we do not control. There are people want us dead already. Billy Phillips never helped anybody in all my life. If I do not help now, Billy will never get another shot. I want to tell you who Billy Phillips is so that you will know I have no secrets and am ready to do anything for this work. I will even tell you things I told almost nobody. In my life I have always been selfish. When I start out I even desired our father sexually. I made sure I got him and our family disintegrated. I gave into the dark despair. I never told anybody it was really my fault even when they convinced me it wasn't my fault. I gave into the dark despair because when I was young I liked the thrilling machines and drugs. They were my first Unnatural High. I had a hard time cold turkeying those. Then I became Dazzling Billy making up with wit and hot the hole inside. He was witty and hot alright. He connected with none of all the men he had and made promises to. Half of which are already dead and more dying everyday. Including Billy perhaps. I will tell you something which I never told anyone. I was born to do your work. I lived on the streets of New York and San Francisco nearly half a year.

The paper in my hand grew very small. I held onto the table, then dropped my head between my knees until the galloping darkness went away.

I tried to hurt myself. I looked at lights in windows of tall buildings where rich people worked and lived. I worked in a skyscraper office one day and I fainted. Big stores turned me out. Tricks saw me in the street and ran away before seeing I wasn't asking for anything. I scored and took the bus to San Francisco. Last Chance City. Same New York men. Same Billy. I want this work so badly. These men are me. This is My Last Chance.

I wanted to crawl back into bed and hide for ever. Instead I watched myself prepare to hurt myself, prepare to prove I was a survivor, unlike Billy, and make myself feel how much it hurt, make myself doubt if it was a price worth paying. I put on a pair of shorts and started up the hill towards the park in heat that slowed me down so badly I might have had weights strapped to my hands and knees. There were other runners out even on this day in the searing midday heat when it would have been healthier to stay home. I sorted them automatically, looking for the ones I wanted to be like, the elite men and women who'd train in any temperature, carrying not an ounce of excess fat on their fine bones, light-headed from their obsession. There were beginners, overweight or old, persevering through the first few steps, out in the heat because they didn't know any better; and the in-between runners like me, disciplining themselves in a ritual that had helped keep life bearable for years. I'd been eating breakfast when I started reading Billy's essay, and though I'd soon stopped eating it was 20 years since I'd run with so much food in my belly. Nothing was usual today. I was mesmerized by the revelation of his pain.

This is the way I'd chosen to remember Billy. Even when he disliked someone, the most he could bring himself to do to them was give a smiling offhand shrug, not dismissing them but letting them go in peaceful coexistence. I knew Billy was strong. I knew Billy knew how to live. *How could he believe he'd never helped anyone?* All the years of trouble were just superficial shit, conflict between Billy and the people who weren't like him, who couldn't bear to be themselves the way Billy was himself and was ready to pay for it. Don't think the essay told me anything about Billy I didn't already know or could have guessed. Don't think Billy and I were really any different. I recognized every word he wrote, except that I was bitterly ashamed I'd learned to put words together properly and he never had. I just hadn't heard the details of how hard it had been for him. But that was his *choice*. He knew I'd always give him money. Judgment free. *Suppose I'd come across another man like Billy in San Francisco - wouldn't I have looked the other way?*

For a long time I seemed to be toiling along in dry air that burned my throat and skin, while I labored under greater pain. How could Billy risk breaking my heart by going on the street? He'd written the essay as though I didn't exist. Well, he'd had his points to get across, maybe he didn't want to dilute the message. Maybe he told Mar what he thought Mar wanted to hear. Maybe a handwriting analyst could tell from his signature how he really felt the day he wrote the essay. Bullshit. Billy had lived his life as if I didn't exist. Knowing he had me wasn't enough to stop him going on the terrible streets beneath the high buildings where I worked and lived. He behaved as if he had nothing, while I kept my distance, relatively safe, very willing to believe we were still close.

I noticed that my movements had become fluid and stronger. Sweat flowed off my upper body and soaked my shorts. I noted that the good feeling of lonely physical effort eased the mind into comfortable thoughts as usual: *All you'll ever know about Billy is what you choose to believe you know. The essay is one piece of evidence, written for a purpose that had nothing to do with you. He was stronger than he appears in the essay, strong enough for Mar or his cronies to need to kill him. What would Billy say to you now if he were alive? Wouldn't he still be the brother who'd have killed to protect you?*

But I felt I didn't deserve to be comforted by the softening of the pain Billy had suffered. I thought I'd already started to die when Billy died; I grew even colder at the thought of how little I'd allowed myself to love him.

An elite runner in the red and white Athletics West uniform eased his way past me on the dirt path, his feet barely touching the ground, every cell of his body fueled by a purity of intention, a simplicity of means, that would always be beyond my grasp. The price didn't seem worth paying.

Chapter Twenty Two

THE EVALUATION SCALE on Billy's application form purported to assess the extent of Billy's "self-realization" on a scale of 1 to 10 before and after the transfer. Before, someone had circled a 2. After, a 6. For a while I mentally circled numbers when I found myself thinking of certain people. Shannon? A 5+. Wink? A 7. Mar? Probably a 9, presuming you were willing to suspend judgment about the self he'd realized. Myself? Don't ask.

"What are you really upset about?" Luke asked on the phone. "That Mar's getting it on with clients? Or that he's getting it on with street people with AIDS? Or that they're black?"

"Probably all of the above," I said. "But that's not the point. Where I come from you do not screw around with people you're paid to take care of. And you don't do drugs with them."

"You don't know that that's the case," Luke said. "You're programed to see drugs in places they don't exist."

"Mar was stoned, at the very least," I said.

"Let me see. It would be all right for you to fuck a client who came to you with legal problems, but not for Mar to fuck," Luke hooted, "excuse me, get fucked by, a terminally-ill client at the Dormitory."

I was getting angrier. "It's different," I said. "Apart from the public health problem. The clients at the Dormitory are vulnerable in all sorts of ways. They should be treated respectfully. They shouldn't be sexual fodder for Marlin Golding."

"What does it really matter?" Luke asked. "These men are going to die. If they want to have some fun with Mar –"

"It's hard for me to believe we're really having this argument, Luke. The whole situation is a mess. Mar doing drugs with a client? My God!"

"You don't know that!"

"First," I said, starting to feel like a schoolteacher rapping Luke's knuckles, "Mar should look for sexual partners outside work. He shouldn't be screwing people he's paid to look after. Second, it's really bad for morale at the Dormitory that some of the clients are being used for sex."

"One client, maybe, as far as you know," Luke said.

"I *know*. There could be all kinds of tensions and problems with favoritism. And if the clients are wondering if they're going to get laid, how can they work on real issues with Shannon or the volunteers? Like getting off drugs?"

"Maybe one of their issues is wanting to get laid."

I groaned. "The whole operation is sleazy and opportunistic. Untrained, unsupervised people doing intrusive things on volunteers' heads and getting away with it because they're in the middle of an epidemic. Mar's boyfriend handling finances."

"It's simple nepotism. When he got money, Mar gave jobs to the people he wanted to have around."

"Why are you defending him? Does the San Francisco gay world operate on a different value frequency from the rest of America?"

"Wake up and smell the coffee," Luke said. "You really were in a drunken stupor for 20 years." I was so taken aback that I hardly heard what he said next. I was accustomed to the sort of uproarious self-flagellation we engaged in at A.A. meetings, but not to having other people use my past against me – particularly not drinkers like Luke. But even when I was angry with Luke I found it easy to forgive him.

"Look at what goes on in local and federal government and the White House. The Reagan administration and the City of New York did their best to ignore AIDS for five long years. The Centers for Disease Control and the National Institutes of Health swore for years the government was giving them all the money they needed to fight the disease. It took access to their papers under the Freedom of Information Act and interrogation under oath to get them to admit they couldn't move for lack of funds while thousands of Americans were dying. All you're talking about at the Factory is a little sex and people who don't bother to work at keeping up the appearance of propriety. Mar's Factory is a private organization that can basically do what it wants as long as they don't break laws, and the Dormitory can do the same as long as they fulfil their contracts with the city."

"Maybe I really don't belong in this town," I sighed, exasperated. "Rule number one where I come from is that when you're entrusted with people's care you do not abuse them, sexually or emotionally or physically. That applies whether you're straight or gay."

"Maybe you ought to give the Dormitory clients the benefit of the doubt and assume they can take care of themselves."

"Of course they can't," I said. "They're homeless addicts with a —" (I caught myself in time) "— potentially terminal disease. Their entire situation implies severe social and personality dysfunction. To tell you the truth, I hate Mar's whole touchy-feely approach. He sentimentalizes the clients at the same time as he exploits them. The clients need to get clean, not have some middle-class volunteer turn himself inside out trying to share their mind space. Though I suppose if Mar concentrated just on getting them clean fewer clients would come to the Dormitory and then there'd be no jobs for Mar and his cronies. Not that the place was overflowing last night."

"Mar isn't a drug rehab expert."

"He's not any kind of expert."

"Mar and the Dormitory workers are the only group who've been willing to make a major effort to work with homeless addicted PWAs on a daily basis," Luke reiterated. "Without him they'd be on the street with occasional stops at Central Emergency to get patched up for more wars. Or they'd get the runaround from the other agencies that are supposed to work with the homeless but draw the line at Mar's kind of client. You know nothing about the way this city works. Who the hell are you to criticize the Dormitory?"

"I don't trust them," I said. "I know they had something to do with Billy's death."

"Proof?"

"They're shifty and cautious when I try to talk about it."

"That may be your imagination. A little paranoia in a recovering drunk. I think you're betting on Mar because he's all you've turned up."

I was willing to admit that much to myself, but not to Luke. "Jerry the barber is suspicious too. It was Jerry who directed me to the Factory. He said they aren't to be trusted and they were shunning Billy. But leave Billy out of it. Those people are still sleazy adventurers."

"Maybe it takes adventurers to do that kind of work," Luke said. "All the experts want a piece of the AIDS action, but on their terms. They want to keep their hands clean and they want to do their own thing and make AIDS patients fit into their agendas. You should have seen psychiatrists jumping in at the very beginning of the epidemic, the way they try to jump in everywhere, trying to do therapy and running groups for AIDS patients. They treated them like psych patients, not ordinary men and women with a physical illness." (I noticed that Luke always referred to PWAs as "them," not "us.") "I've sat in on an AIDS group run by a gay psychiatrist who refused to tell the men in the group that he was gay, who refused to reveal anything about himself, who sat there waiting for those men to reveal themselves so that he could shrink them."

"Shrinks are doctors who couldn't make it in any other specialty," I said. "But that's not what we're talking about."

"I interviewed a social worker at the AIDS clinic who told me she thought *everyone* could benefit from psychotherapy," Luke said. "She's spent the last four years building a network of therapists she refers PWAs to. She's done enough favors to assure herself of a job for the next 30 years. That's despite the fact that 90% of the 'therapists' in the city are barely qualified to do an intake interview. Do you think all the best talent in the city rushed into AIDS jobs when the epidemic started? The jobs went to the previously underemployed. There's AIDS money in this city available to every hustler who knows how to make the right pitch to people at the Health Department, who had no qualifications for *their* jobs, except knowing where to look for the list of city jobs created to deal with the epidemic. Once a project gets AIDS funding its main business becomes to justify getting even more money. The Health Department is under pressure to give the funds to the medical establishment or the people with connections, even if their ideas are only marginally effective. The reason an outsider like Marlin Golding at the Dormitory managed to get funding is that he's providing an essential service to people nobody else wanted to touch, and doing it more cheaply than the city had supposed possible. The therapists and counselors and social workers in the AIDS industry are happy to charge the city to evaluate the two per cent of Mar's clients who can stay clean and coherent long enough to keep an appointment at the therapists' convenience."

"I'm not going to get any help from you," I said.

"I'll help you if you show me any evidence that Mar had anything to do with Billy's death. Frankly I think it's a ridiculous idea."

"Why? Because they run the Dormitory? You think murder is a profession that excludes faith healers and people who work with AIDS victims?"

"We don't call them victims in San Francisco," Luke said. "We call them people with AIDS. As it happens I'm interviewing Mar on *Head to Head* on Sunday morning. If you have any revelations please tell me so that I can confront Mar live."

"The maze is a potential death trap," I said.

Pause. "Yes, it is," Luke said. "He could lose city funding over that, and it's exactly the sort of thing inexperienced people like the Dormitory workers would overlook when they were converting the bathhouse. I'll go down there with a cameraman."

"And Mar sharing drugs with clients?"

"I won't raise that unless you have some proof," Luke said. "I won't hurt the work."

Chapter Twenty Three

THE BALANCE SHEET prepared by a local accounting firm carried the disclaimer that it was based on a limited review of the Dormitory's books. I was surprised at the amount of money involved: nearly $500,000 a year, most of it from the city, and most of that for staff salaries. Dormitory workers were well paid on average, but there was no breakdown. Mar and Shannon and Wink could each have been paid $50,000 and a part-time cook $3,000. I had to assume that city overseers kept the salaries within reason and that I'd have to look elsewhere for financial corruption.

The newsletter Wink had given me contained a public relations Q & A session with Mar which sought to lay at rest continuing rumors of a connection between the Factory and the Dormitory. I thought it was deeply dishonest. The patients who came to the Factory for deliverance and the volunteers who took part in the transfer at the Dormitory both submitted to a form of brainwashing; a kind of zonked subservience to Mar seeped into every corner of the operations.

If Mar was on the take in a major way it had to be from gifts to the Factory – with which the city wasn't involved – or in the misappropriation of private money coming into the Dormitory. One of Mar's answers in the P.R. handout had to do with his helping fund the Dormitory with Factory money. He said that after deduction of minor operating expenses all gifts to the Factory were rechannelled to keep the Dormitory going. He mentioned no amounts in the interview, but private gifts to the

Dormitory were listed at $78,000 on the balance sheet.

I called a San Francisco financial consultant my former partners in New York had used and asked him if he could get access to more detailed financial reports at City Hall. He groaned when I mentioned Marlin Golding; I thought my suspicions were about to be confirmed.

"It isn't that these places are deliberately dishonest," he said. "But they're used to operating on a shoestring. When they suddenly get money they're an accountants' nightmare because they have no procedures established for tracking or reporting income."

He agreed to let an assistant do some digging if I'd pay her the equivalent of two weeks of a summer intern's salary.

Chapter Twenty Four

I GOT SO few calls that each time the phone rang I thought it must be one of Billy's friends who didn't know he was dead.

"This is Lev."

"Hi," I said, not identifying myself.

"I believe you're a friend of Jerry's. The barber."

I remembered the bearded man at the meeting who'd eventually given me Jerry's number. "You introduced me to him," I said.

Pause. He laughed uncomfortably. "Well, I found your number in his book so you must have gotten to know him."

"I did. He's helped me a lot. And he gave me a gay haircut. I didn't know he was doing it until it was too late."

Pause. Something formal about the call had started to worry me.

"The reason I called is that a friend and I split his address book down the middle and agreed each of us would call half the names."

Pause. In the shift of a moment I found myself in the dead space that precedes inevitable bad news; part of me wanted to roll back time and avoid the inevitable; part of me rushed towards a cheap thrill.

"Did you know that Jerry died the day before yesterday?" Lev asked.

"No," I said, feeling deadened. I let the appropriate words flow automatically, displacing whatever feeling I might have had.

"I could tell he was very sick. I wondered how he managed to keep cutting hair at all." I saw Jerry standing in front of me, pointing his comb for effect, his bruised eye slightly squinty, the purple ball on the end of his nose isolating him, signaling how limited his choices had become. Everyone kept dying.

"He needed the money," Lev was saying.

Yes. "Did he die in the hospital?"

"No. A client found him. He'd left his front door open."

"I'm sorry he died alone," I said. "I hope he wasn't in pain."

Pause. "Not when he died," Lev said. "I think he chose to avoid any more pain."

I wasn't sure what to say.

"Lots of men make that choice," Lev continued. "Everyone knows the Hemlock recipe now. Any San Francisco doctor will give you the ingredients at separate times if you humor him and describe the right symptoms. The death will be ascribed to cardiac failure, which is how Jerry would have died anyway when the internal lesions kept spreading."

"I wish he hadn't had to die alone," I said.

Pause. "He didn't have to," Lev said. "He didn't have a lot of friends but he had two or three good ones. Jerry told me he wanted to choose when he died. John my lover, who's making the other half of these calls, and I both said we'd like to be with him when he made the journey. I talked to him the day before he died and he gave no indication he was ready. He may just have decided it was time and he didn't want any of our drama. Who knows what was going through his head?"

"Who knows what people think about when they're about to die," I said.

"How long are you going to be in San Francisco?"

"Indefinitely," I said. "Lev, let me ask you something. Did Jerry ever mention anything about Marlin Golding at the Factory to you? I think he must have since you gave me his number in connection with Billy's death."

Pause. "Jerry was fairly paranoid about the Factory and the Dormitory," Lev said. "Most people are if they ever work there and leave. They're guilty because it's like deserting brothers in need. I think they invent reasons for blaming Marlin Golding instead of themselves. But Jerry never mentioned Marlin being involved in your brother's death. In fact it sounds ridiculous to

134

me. I think Jerry was upset about the sexual shenanigans."

"You mean Mar going to bed with clients?"

"No," Lev said. "I know nothing about that. I meant Mar and the other staff members. Everybody knows Mar's way of getting to know someone is to go to bed with them. Jerry was an old-fashioned gay man. He thought men should only go to bed with men."

"You mean Mar and Shannon?"

"There are other women on the staff and there are women volunteers. I think Mar finds it easier to get the women into bed than the men. Most gay men find him kind of repulsive."

"Lev, forgive me, but some of what you're saying doesn't make sense to me. I came to that A.A. meeting to find out how Billy died. I thought that was why you gave me your number. I thought that was why you gave me Jerry's number later on."

"I knew Jerry had met Billy at the Dormitory," Lev said.

"How did you know?"

Pause. "I think he mentioned giving Billy a haircut."

"Jerry never told me that," I said.

"Anyway," Lev said, "I thought he might know something, or at least put your mind at rest. If I really felt there was anything sinister going on there I wouldn't work there two nights a week. That's where John and I met. Will you promise that you won't mention to anyone that I talked to you? There is some paranoia at the Dormitory because a lot of people are out to get Mar. People are jealous because he came from nowhere suddenly and now he has all this power and money. There's always jealousy around AIDS power and money. Everyone thinks they should be doing more themselves and they think any money should go directly to patients. But that's not the way it seems to work. The money goes mostly to healthy people who are paid to provide services for PWA's."

"I promise," I said, thinking that perhaps there were things that worried Lev he hadn't admitted even to himself. "Have you been in the maze, Lev?"

Silence.

"There's a maze on the third floor that the clients could easily get lost in."

"I've hardly ever been up there," Lev said. "I work mostly in the kitchen."

"I think it's a leftover from the bathhouse days," I said.

"I hardly ever went to bathhouses," Lev said.

I ran downstairs to answer the knocking on the door that afternoon because I thought it might be the mailman with bills I'd asked my sponsor to forward from Minneapolis. I'd stopped answering the front door at night after I dealt with two men knocking at the right number on the wrong street and three drug buyers ready to blame me because their contact wasn't answering next door.

"I told you he was in," the young woman standing in the next doorway said to a serene young man. She didn't look at me. I saw pride in her profile, stubborn denial, a determination to handle it herself, supposing she'd admitted there was something wrong. Rather than look at me she turned inside her house the unnatural way – facing the blank wall next to the door handle – so that she'd have to lean backwards to close the door behind her.

"I'm from PG&E," the young man said, "and I'm here about the weather proofing program to conserve energy. I already talked to the landlord and the neighbors."

I stepped back to let him inside.

"That we could fix," he said, pointing to a two-inch gap at the bottom of the door. "Have you just moved in?" he asked when he saw the empty front rooms upstairs. "Do you have a loft?"

I showed him a trap door in the ceiling over the refrigerator.

"There's probably a very shallow space and another door directly onto the roof," he said. "We'd certainly want to look at that."

I took him into the living room and showed him the broken window sash. "Oh my," he said. "We'd certainly fix that. This program is for landlords with lower income tenants. Your neighbors qualify because they're unemployed."

I'd noticed that my neighbors had two cars, one of them usually parked on the sidewalk outside the house.

"May I ask if you're employed?"

"Not at the moment," I said. "By the way, the PG&E bill for this apartment is under $10 a month. You wouldn't be saving much energy."

"Would you like to complete the paperwork now?" he asked.

"I'd be happy to look at it," I said.

He handed me a yellow form with the qualifying guidelines: One tenant – Less than $6,000 annual income.

"I don't qualify," I said. "Nobody who lived here could qualify. The rent is nearly $6,000 a year." I wondered what rental income the landlord reported.

"Have you been living here long?" he asked.

"Only a few weeks. I stayed on in the apartment when my brother died."

"What was your brother's income?" he asked.

"Clearly more than $6,000 since he paid the same amount of rent. I'm afraid I don't qualify for your program."

"If you like we could come to an arrangement," he said, his face quite bland.

"Sorry," I said. "I'm afraid not. I file tax returns. Sorry to waste your time." I handed the form back to him. "What do you really want?"

He blinked twice, nodded, put away his papers, and preceded me downstairs with admirable composure.

Chapter Twenty Five

"HI, I'M VALERIE O'Connor. I knew your brother Billy."

Her voice was young and practiced at being bright and warm. "I used to work at the Dormitory," she said.

I wondered what they were up to now. "Let me take you to dinner," I said.

She laughed. "All right," she said, and began to make hesitating sounds about when.

"Tonight," I said.

She laughed again. "Tonight is my Course in Miracles. How about Friday?"

"All right. Tell me where to pick you up."

"Come here at 7:30," she said. "I'll make dinner. It'll be quieter here."

"The maze is blocked off," Luke said. "Mar says he blocked it off before they opened the Dormitory. That has to be true. They had city inspectors there."

"He's lying," I said. "Couldn't you tell the carpentry was just done?"

"The entrances were blocked with metal drums," Luke said.

"They could have picked those up anywhere in that industrial area south of Market. What about the hole Edwin knocked in the wall?"

Luke hesitated. "I didn't see that."

"Did you look for it?"

"It would have proved nothing. It could have been made

anytime. The point is that the entrances are blocked off."

"Don't you believe me, Luke?"

"I believe what you told me about the maze," he said. "They got to it before us."

This is what I went to Valerie's house hoping for: that her warmth would be genuine, that her motives would be benign, that she'd known Billy well and would be able to bring him back to life for me for a short time, that I might even find lasting comfort with her. I too was looking for miracles.

She lived in a white two-story apartment building in the avenues north of Golden Gate Park. The heat of the day had retreated around five o'clock – it seemed impossible to predict when it would last through the night – and cold fog filmed and flared the street lamps and the lights I saw through the windows of people's houses. It pricked my face in a thousand places when I got out of the taxi. A blind man might have thought at first that it was raining, but my face stayed damp, not wet.

Valerie greeted me with the healthy cheerfulness of a woman who knows she will always make a good first impression. She was beautiful. She was tall and slim, with long black hair pulled behind her head and pale slightly freckled Irish skin. Her eyes were large and green and had no trouble meeting mine; her mouth was long and smooth. She seemed to like me on first sight, and to bring intelligence and judgment to that liking. I suppose she was over 30, but she reminded me of a woman ten years younger whom every man in my law school class wanted, although she'd made it clear she'd already chosen a highly suitable partner and wasn't dumb enough to rock the boat.

I handed Valerie a bottle of good wine at the door and she immediately busied herself with opening it. A quick look around the room confirmed that I still couldn't accuse anyone I met in San Francisco of being house-proud: the furniture was adequate but sparse and ordinary. Valerie had hung something on the walls but I can't remember what, because it wasn't worth looking at. There was hardly a book or record in sight.

I followed her into the kitchen from habit to catch her in time; I knew she'd assume I wanted some of the wine. It smelled strong and heady as she splashed it into a glass. The liquid sound and the warm color brought back memories of years of quick comfort. As usual, I thought: Why not?

"Not for me," I said. Maybe this time the desire was a little harder to put down. But I always worried about that.

She looked surprised. "It smells wonderful," she said. "Won't you have a little?"

"Not for me," I said. "I'm allergic to alcohol."

Valerie seemed disappointed, but maybe she was only worried about what else she had to offer me. She opened the refrigerator.

"I have Seven Up and grapefruit juice."

"Juice will be fine. What is the Course in Miracles?"

"It's a kind of therapeutic spiritual journey." She smiled without a trace of mockery. "I just joined a study group that meets once a week."

I was used to seeing this kind of resourceful intelligence brought to bear on matters of law or science, not the search for Band-Aids for ordinary human pain. But I wasn't supposed to entertain such thoughts; the program taught me not to make fun of spiritual quests.

Valerie led me into the main room again and sat close and facing me on the couch, cupping her wine glass in both hands, her eyes glowing. She searched my face. "Have you reached some sort of closure over Billy's death?"

My heart sank. Why was this city full of people who talked like eager and inept would-be therapists?

"No," I said angrily. "I never want to reach closure over Billy's death. I want it to hurt me until the day I die. I hope I die thinking about him."

Valerie opened her mouth to respond but thought better of it. "He was a very lovable man," she said.

"He was so lovable that nobody in this city where he lived for 20 years seems to know anything about him," I said. "They're dead or they've moved or they're not talking for some reason. He must have meant a great deal to whoever murdered him. Somebody knew him well enough to know he had something worth breaking into his apartment for."

This time Valerie took her time to reply. "Of course I know nothing about that," she said, "but I think I did know him rather well."

"Then tell me about the Billy you knew," I said.

She nodded, thought, drank her wine, and got up. "I'll be back in three minutes," she said. I heard her moving about in the kitchen and watched her bring in a salad bowl and some plates and set them on the dining table by the windows with white nylon curtains. She seemed nervous about the table and the food. She took a red pillar candle out of a drawer and lit it – I wondered if former Dormitory associates got a discount, or perhaps a box of six as a parting gift – and returned and sat close to me again holding a full glass of wine. She drank from it gratefully and set it on the carpet.

She let me watch her searching for the right words: this was to be an event. "Billy was so – open," she said. She was close enough for me to smell the wine on her breath. And she mimicked Billy's openness with shining searching eyes and parted lips, cocking her head to one side as she waited for inspiration. "It was always incredible to me that he'd experienced so much and could still open his heart to new learning and new feelings." I noticed the gap where a tooth was missing in the left side of her mouth. Her front teeth were rather prominent, which I hadn't allowed myself to see at first. I thought, what is wrong with me that I look for flaws in this beautiful woman?

But I was so disappointed at her foolishness that I began to be certain she'd brought me here to deceive or use me. "What did Billy open himself to?" I asked, feeling grim.

"To the possibility of feeling pain again," she said easily. "His own pain and other people's. I think he'd closed his heart, as so many people have. But the AIDS crisis empowered him to start growing again."

I kept hearing the same words and phrases repeated by anyone connected with the Dormitory. I felt a flash of fury at these people who presumed to talk about my brother's emotional growth. "Do you have any specific memories of Billy?" I asked. "Things he said? Things that were going on in his life?"

Valerie seemed irritated at being checked and brought back to earth. She showed an earthier side. "I don't think he had a boy friend," she said almost roughly. "A lot of volunteers don't. That's why they have time to nurture and care for the clients. Maybe he did find a boy friend. Maybe that's why he stopped working at the Dormitory." She got up. "I think we can eat now."

Dinner was a pork chop casserole in a bland watery gravy and a salad of iceberg lettuce and tomato. It was like the first attempt at cooking of a woman who'd just gotten her first apartment. I wondered where these people had been, to be starting this late. But Valerie ate her food quickly and with enjoyment.

"Are you still very much involved with the Factory and the Dormitory?" I asked.

She turned harsh. "I was *never* involved with the Factory," she said. Then her face switched expressions and took on a professional radiance. "It's hard to give up involvement with the Dormitory completely. It taps into such deep stuff, needing to be needed by some of the neediest people in the world. It was time for me to move on and take more care of myself. Not many people can handle the intensity of it for long. Mar can. He has some magical way of renewing himself, some secret well of masculine and feminine strengths."

I thought better of telling her that I hadn't noticed Mar's masculine side. I wondered how an intelligent woman could make such a pretentious fool of herself.

"How long have you known Mar?" I asked.

She smiled a sentimental smile, her cheeks flushed with the wine she'd drunk so quickly. "Mar and I go back a long way," she said.

I felt the back of my neck turn cold, as if I'd connected with mortal danger. Billy's murder, not just his death, felt close to me. "Shannon said exactly the same thing," I said.

Valerie's mouth tightened, just as Shannon's had. She looked away – there was nothing in the room for her to really look at, so she started getting ready to move into the kitchen again – and as I watched her I realized how near to me she was across the small table. She wore a green blouse which clung softly to her small breasts.

"Was the maze left open when you worked at the Dormitory?" I asked.

"The maze?" She was full of surprise as if the question was totally unexpected. "Of course not. That would be very dangerous."

"Just how was it closed off?"

She thought for a moment and drank some wine, so obviously playing for time that I knew she'd been briefed by Mar. But not fully. "How?"

"Yeah, how was it closed off? Was it boarded up? Did they seal the entrance with bricks? *How*?"

"I think it was boarded up," she said, getting up. "I'll be back in a moment." She took her wine glass with the dinner plates. When she returned with more plates and a bowl of strawberries she brought back her wine glass, filled this time with white wine. She left again and returned with a Mr. Coffee pot. "It doesn't matter how it was closed off," she said. "I know the moment Mar saw it he knew it had to be sealed off for the sake of the clients."

At least I was certain now that she was a liar.

"Were there any clients at the Dormitory who Billy might have gotten particularly involved with?" I pressed.

"That's one of the heartbreaking things about working at the Dormitory," Valerie said rather wearily. "The clients come and go. If they're too sick to leave by themselves we lose them to Central Emergency or General. Some of them come for one night and we never see them again. And street people are hard to get to know anyway, even when they're not drugged or dying. If it was easy for them to form ties with others they might not be street people."

I realized how easy it was for Valerie and her former colleagues to sit back and let the reality of the situation at the Dormitory thwart me.

"The last time I was at the Dormitory there was a client taking a shower in the middle of the afternoon," I said. "Have you any idea what he was doing there if you never let the clients in until six o'clock?"

"I don't know what that particular man was doing there," she said easily. "We have to have rules to ease the burden on the workers and establish realistic expectations for the clients. That doesn't mean we won't break the rules to help someone if we can. Maybe he had an interview about permanent housing and we wanted him to look in good shape."

"I wonder what draws people to impossible work?" I asked, although I was sure I knew. The candlelight and the smell of Valerie's wine and the intensity of my search and the possibility that Valerie was physically available to me were starting to make me feel drunk. I wanted to fuck her, and comfort and love had nothing to do with it any more.

"I suppose the challenge," she said, her eyes glittering. "The excitement of working on the front lines, although the idea is actually more exciting than the day-to-day reality. The publicity is certainly flattering. I never thought I'd do anything people would interview me about."

I liked her when she was honest. "That's not quite what I meant," I said. "I don't think it even makes sense to ask why a lot of people get involved. People fit the normal curve. You can expect to find the usual small number of charlatans and murderers and Mother Theresas. But I think Marlin Golding does what he does because he has very few choices. He could be some obscure counterculture figure living on unemployment or welfare and whatever he can hustle, or he can run the Dormitory. How much does he pay himself?"

Valerie looked worried. But she'd drunk at least a bottle of wine and maybe she was having trouble thinking quite clearly. "About $40,000, the last time I heard," she said unwillingly.

"And there must be perks," I said. "A plane ticket now and then from someone who's grateful to him, a deal on a car or an apartment. It's a one-man private organization, so he doesn't have to be particularly scrupulous." Valerie was listening hard. "But even if all he earns is $40,000 a year, that's far more than he could ever really have expected to earn in a regular job with no training or education or background. My question is, how was Marlin able to seize the opportunity, to take the risk?"

"Mar is an extraordinary man," Valerie said firmly.

"I think he's very ordinary, in some ways less than ordinary. The opportunity was available to him because nobody else wanted it. Nobody else wanted impossible heartbreaking work. I think Mar took it on because he didn't even have the normal realistic expectations that everybody else has, because he had nothing to lose. He might as well try for everything. I'm certain of that, because Mar thinks and behaves like an alcoholic. Which I am, by the way."

Valerie's eyes strayed towards her wine glass, but she stopped herself in time.

"I recognize his grandiosity," I went on, "the refusal to be bound by normal limits, the lack of even knowing what normal limits are. I know Mar inside out."

She tried reason. "Does it matter why Mar does it, or who he is, as long as those people's needs are being met?"

"It's not just a service. Everything that goes on at the Dormitory and the Factory is influenced by who Mar is. He plays with the clients' and volunteers' deepest needs and hopes. The transfer is deeply intrusive. It gives Mar a mine of private information that could be used against the volunteers. Apparently he's fucked or been fucked by half the people who work for him. It's a deeply corrupt system. Why did you switch jobs, Valerie? So that you could spread the gospel and grease Mar's path at City Hall?"

She blinked – it was like a tic – and raised her glass with a defiant look at me and gulped her wine. "You make it sound like a conspiracy, and that's ridiculous."

"Maybe. I don't think so. I hear the same words parroted by so many people, as if you'd been programed. You don't all have to say 'ridiculous.' There's crazy and absurd and ludicrous and preposterous."

She shrugged away what I said, looking close to tears, and took her wine glass and went and sat on the couch. I followed her.

"All I know," Valerie said, "is that thousands of human beings are dying, and hundreds of them are hungry and on the streets." Her lower lip started to tremble. "Nobody ought to die like that."

She sat there with the cross expression of someone about to cry, trying to manufacture tears in a kind of vulgar hysteria. I believed that unless you were drunk, or trying to create emotion so that you could exploit it, you didn't cry over people you didn't know. You cried for yourself, or your own. And if you had no one of your own, that was probably due to your own self- absorbed heart.

"Why did you really leave the Dormitory, Valerie? Because Mar had moved on to Wink or Shannon or somebody else? Did something happen you couldn't live with?"

I'd sat close enough to her that our feet were touching. I didn't like the spoiled anger I saw in her face, and I kept looking down at her breasts that seemed to have swelled but were still soft inside the green blouse. She was definitely wearing a bra, but something minimal that I could get off in a second.

Valerie met my eyes. Her own eyes were tearful but she was also mocking me. "It's really none of your business," she said.

As soon as I moved towards her Valerie reached out and pulled my head closer, but she was cold and angry. I had a raging hard-on that had gotten painfully tied up in the brief I was wearing. This is what I wanted: I wanted her beautiful clean scented body to respond to mine so that I knew she wanted to give it to me; I wanted her to let me see and touch her body that she wanted to reveal to me, I wanted to uncover her warm breasts and touch them and lick her nipples so that she moaned; and finally when I had her naked except for her panties I wanted to put my hand down there so that when I pulled them off and put my finger inside her I knew there was no one else whose cock she wanted but mine, that she wanted my big cock pushing through her and keeping going until she was all open to me and screaming and ready for the load I'd empty inside her.

I smelled the wine which had turned sour on her breath. Her body was like ice, as if she was sick or terrified. Immediately I wanted to surround her with my body to warm and comfort her but she held my shoulders away from her as I reached my mouth towards hers. Kissing her was like trying to contact a woman who wasn't there, even as she moved her lower body under me and thrust against my crotch to tell me I could have her. I tried to kiss her face, lick the sides of her nose and her eyelids and bury my face in her neck so that our bodies comforted each other, but she pushed her mouth back on mine and nipped my lower lip with her teeth. I met her eyes an inch away and saw in them what might have been taken for the challenge of passion, but it looked to me as if she despised me. So I was left with a hard-on and the chance of a fuck to get rid of it while the rest of my body might as well have been someplace else. It was like using a second-class whore again. Undressing her wasn't like getting a chance to show a woman how wonderful she was, how grateful I was to be given her. I pulled her little breasts out of her bra in a second and ran my thumbs over the nipples, but there was no special uncovering about it, it was only like saying, Now we both know exactly where we're going and what we're going to get. I felt the moment when Valerie lost whatever it was about her that interested me in Valerie and became cunt. I felt all unselfish feeling leave me. I ground my crotch against her for a moment, just to let her know what to expect, one of my hands inside her jeans completely holding her ass under me it was so small. Then I pulled off her jeans and stood over her lying on the couch in her panties. I signalled that we should open up the bed but she shook her head. So I pulled off her panties, me still with my clothes on, and let her know what she was. I pulled her thighs up so that she was upside down, her shoulders on the couch and her black hair dragged out behind her head, and pulled her legs apart and raised her cunt into the light and stood there exposing it and opening it up roughly with two or three thrusts of the fingers of one hand while she gasped, while I balanced her upside down. I reached down and pulled her shoulders up against mine and held her face opposite mine one last time. She looked at me with a kind of triumph and contempt. I opened my mouth and moved it towards her mouth but she jerked her head away. I laid her back on the couch and took my clothes off, except for my T-shirt. One thing, I think, has kept me feeling as if I belong in this world: I feel comfortable in my body, I'm proud of my cock and balls.

"You don't need that," she said, Valerie again, when she saw me taking the packet out of my jacket pocket. She laughed. "I'm sure you don't have any diseases."

I didn't tell her it was her I was afraid of, spending so much time with AIDS patients and probably fucking Mar and his friends. "I've been carrying two of Billy's rubbers since my second day in San Francisco," I said. "This is the first chance I've had to use one."

I went over and straddled her again, looming over her while I fitted the rubber over the swollen head of my cock and rolled it on. Valerie looked really angry and somehow thwarted.

I felt sober again. A lot of the violence and the excitement had gone. My head was clear and I just needed to take care of my cock.

What a relief to fit it into her cunt which I held suspended between my fingers, not quickly but in a smooth thrust that she had no chance of stalling or pulling away from. She grunted.

"Oh yeah," I said, and gathered her ass around my cock. "You're gonna like this. Your pussy was just made for this big dick."

She held herself pushing skewered onto me but she balanced herself on her shoulders and started climbing her feet up my chest and onto my shoulders. It didn't fit with what I was doing,

147

trying to get really at home inside her and get a rhythm going. While I was still trying to do that she started hitting my ears with her feet and then her feet were on my face and I realized she was trying to dig her toenails into my face. I pulled her feet away from my face and pushed her knees back beside her head while she fought against me.

"I'll give you all the excitement you can handle inside your cunt," I said. "We don't need any extras. What did Mar use to fuck you? His fingers?"

Valerie screamed at me and her shoulders reared towards me and she started tearing at my chest through the shirt with her fingernails. I threw her away. The head of the rubber stuck inside her when she pulled her legs together as I came out of her and she fell sideways but I grabbed it with my fingers and it stayed on my cock glistening and intact as I stood up and turned away from her.

"Fuck you," she said. "You think you know how to make me happy? It's like fucking a machine."

"You'll do a lot better with me than some of the men you know," I said, starting to pull off the rubber. "I used to pay for this kind of scene. I don't want to do it any more."

An idea about someone's plan was starting to form in my head. The scratches on my chest stung and there were scrapes of blood on my shirt. My face felt swollen. Valerie sat up and held out her hand for the rubber. I shook my head and folded the rubber into a handkerchief. Still nearly naked, I picked up the telephone.

"Who are you calling?" Valerie cried.

"Yellow Cab," I said.

"Get a cab outside," she cried.

"No way," I said.

I dialled her number as soon as I got home. It was busy, as I'd expected.

I dialled Luke's number. He answered on the third ring.

"I think Mar and his friends tried to set me up," I said. "Did you ever meet Valerie O'Connor?"

"I think she was working at the Dormitory when I did the report."

"She invited me to her house and it ended up looking

suspiciously like a rape scene."

Pause. "I've been home all evening," Luke said. "You can say you were with me."

"I can't ask you to perjure yourself," I said. "I have a better idea."

I dialled Valerie's number seven or eight times until it was free. She answered on the first ring.

"For your own sake don't hang up," I said.

"I don't want to talk to you."

"Just listen. For your own good. I dropped off the rubber at the police lab. They're going to do an analysis of the vaginal secretions on it. If you people try accusing me of rape my attorney will insist on having a sample taken from you and compare it with what they found on the rubber. They can determine with 95% probability whether it came from the same woman. When it matches you'll have to come up with a convincing explanation of why I stopped to put on a rubber in the middle of raping you."

"You're crazy," Valerie said. "I don't know what you're talking about."

"The cab driver is willing to testify on my behalf. I relayed the whole story on the way home."

She laughed. "Nobody would believe anything he said."

"The cab driver was a woman. A very attractive lesbian with long blonde hair."

"You're crazy and sick," Valerie said.

"I'm on to you," I said. "I'm on to you and Mar and the rest of you. And I'm going to get you. I'm going to get revenge for Billy. I'm going to destroy you."

I hung up, waited two minutes, and dialled Valerie's number again. It was busy again, as I'd expected. I hung up, took the rubber out of the handkerchief, dropped it between two paper towels, sealed it in a plastic bag and put it in the freezer. I had no idea whether I was saving evidence that might be useful to me. I was a corporate attorney; I'd never had anything to do with forensic chemistry in my life. The cab driver had been male, Asian, and about 60 years old.

Chapter Twenty Six

IN THE FINANCIAL district office workers endured the heat wave and the appearance of democracy still prevailed. A bike messenger and a clerk/typist had the same right of way as a hot shot young financier on his way to gently prod a new client into an IPO; a young black in a wheelchair tied up an ATM for seven minutes punching the keys at random and nobody in the line complained (outward propriety, inward seething); a Hispanic truck driver spat his gum to within three inches of my head; a woman struck by a sudden thought stopped dead in the middle of the lunchtime sidewalk and 10 pedestrians braked and shuffled to avoid tripping over each other. I turned round to see how many people had collided behind me. There was no one except a man in a green jacket who suddenly turned into a bookstore without seeming to really look where he was going. It occurred to me that they were following me. After that, until I got tired doing it, I'd look back suddenly or retrace my steps around a corner. But I never surprised anyone else.

If you didn't really want to notice you'd see no sign in the rather well-dressed crowd of the epidemic consuming thousands a few blocks away, but I knew better by now. I saw the young men in business suits whose skin was reddened and dry, and it looked subtly different from the results of too much sun, and other men whose bodies were stripped of fat and muscle and seemed to keep going on determination. I saw them alone in the street, or lunching at *Sweet Max's* with female colleagues, sharing a little of what conventional time was left with women trying to make sense of it all. In the blue metal boxes full of the magazines and newspapers that get all their income from advertising, they were giving away a 24-page glossy full color publication entitled *Why Does God Allow Suffering?* I walked past it then said what the hell and went back and took a copy. I thought: *I'm even needier than I thought but at least I don't care about people seeing me take it.* But I hid it while I talked to the young woman who'd been investigating Mar's finances.

"If God is all powerful – if he is all love – why does he permit wars, sickness, anguish and pain? Here is the answer to that age-old question." I turned to the end because I couldn't wait for the answer: We're allowed to suffer so that we can earn our eternal reward. This was only what I'd been raised on and elected to put aside these last 40 years. I'd hoped for something I hadn't heard before. Like Valerie, I was still looking for miracles.

Chapter Twenty Seven

HEAD TO HEAD was on at eight o'clock on Sunday morning. I set the alarm and watched it in bed, with Tom pushing his face heavily against my stubble, expecting me to feed him and then perhaps desert him for the day. The program had a gimmick that was unusual enough to get it talked about as a TV innovation in the local press. After the introductory shots of the interviewers and the subject making rather desperate small talk under the titles, the program lived up to its name and filled the screen with the face of whoever was talking: not just a head shot, a face shot — ear to ear, chin to hairline. I'd read hyperbolic comments about the program exposing people's pores and fillings and nose hairs and souls.

In shadowed outline in the opening shots, only the upper half of his body showing above the desk he'd been sat at, Mar's torso looked truncated and misshapen opposite the upper bodies of Luke and the female interviewer, a nightly news anchorwoman. They had smooth, full haircuts while the outline of Mar's head looked like Norman Bates' wig at the end of *Psycho* .

The first close-up of Luke's face was striking: it looked naked and childlike, even though you knew they'd made him up with a layer of shellac. They cut to Mar while Luke was still introducing him and I was shocked by how impressed I was. Of course the gimmick worked in favor of whoever was being scrutinized; you assumed that anyone whose face filled every corner of the screen was worth paying attention to. Mar's self-important little flounces of the head, the ridiculous gracious gestures of his power, were all eliminated. All that was left was a plain face with eyes set too close together, a snub nose, and a narrow mouth with a full upper lip. Rather than mercilessly revealing him, the close-up made Mar seem ordinary and harmless.

The program's second gimmick was that the camera remained focused on the subject's face for the entire 22 minutes. The interviewers even announced commercial breaks in voice over.

"Three years ago nobody had heard of you," Luke's voice said. "Now you head up a shelter for homeless people with AIDS which receives hundreds of thousands of dollars of city money each year. Your Dormitory is being studied by cities like New York and Los Angeles as a possible model for a solution to their AIDS homeless program. Who are you, Marlin Golding? Where did you come from?"

"Not just studied, Luke," Mar said. He was nervous, but working hard at sounding at ease. "I understand that both New York and L.A. are seeking funding to open similar shelters now that they've seen our work." Even his voice sounded regular when he stuck to the simple and concrete. "I'm a San Franciscan, Luke. I was born here and I've lived here all my life except for a period in the late 60's when I went on the road with the civil rights and peace movements, and a year I spent in India."

"What were you doing in San Francisco before AIDS came along?" Luke's voice asked. I paid close attention.

"I worked as a crew member for a documentary filmmaker," Mar said. "I worked as a design assistant in an advertising agency. I volunteered in soup kitchens. I worked for crisis intervention and suicide prevention switchboards."

It was the female interviewer's turn. "Isn't it true that before you started the Dormitory you were working as a faith healer of AIDS patients?" she asked. It was what passed for tough questioning on the program, but she sounded merely chirpy. The interviewers raised an issue that had already been raised elsewhere, then gave the subject plenty of time to present his side.

"I am not now, nor have I ever been a faith healer," Mar said, and paused to smile at his own humor. "Some of the AIDS patients I've been associated with have gone into remission, and that has certainly seemed like a miracle to them and to me. But they deserve all the credit. All I ever did for them was draw their

153

attention to some of the methods men and women all over the world are using to heal themselves of all kinds of diseases."

"What exactly goes on at the Factory?" she asked. I thought Mar couldn't have bought such an opportunity to present his case.

"The Factory is where we meet to meditate and visualize an end to AIDS," Mar said. "The meetings are open to anyone and it's a completely separate operation from the Dormitory, which provides overnight food and housing for homeless PWA's. There's nothing mysterious about what we do at the Factory. Patients tell me their traditional doctors at General and other hospitals encourage them to use our techniques, because they've seen evidence that it helps."

The interviewers started to speak at the same time, but it was Luke's turn. "A persistent comment I've heard about you is that you don't have paper qualifications. You're working with terminally ill patients, but you're not a doctor or a nurse or a scientist."

"You don't need a licence to lead a meditation," Mar said, "which is what I do at the Factory. I've never heard anyone suggest that you need a diploma to serve bed and breakfast to strangers, which is basically what I do at the Dormitory. I grew up in an apartment building that my parents managed and still manage, so I know all about taking care of people. I think the idea that only quote experts unquote should take care of people with AIDS runs counter to all the best thinking in our society. First of all, I don't think there are any true AIDS experts, and if there are, they're certainly not the doctors and scientists who are treating the disease, because they certainly can't cure it. The most they seem to be able to do is make stabs at patching the damage. I think the true AIDS experts are the men and women with the disease, who deal with it intimately 24 hours a day and therefore know more about it than any doctor. They've taken control of their own disease in an unprecedented way, and they've insisted on being in charge of their own treatment and forced doctors to admit exactly what they know and do not know. I think more and more doctors and scientists in our society are being seen as technicians with certain skills. We turn to them for those skills, but we no longer turn to them for comfort or wisdom. The other thing is that AIDS threatens such a large percentage of our population that we can't rely on salaried caregivers to take care of everyone who's sick because it would bankrupt government. There can't be too many people who are as dissimilar as former President Reagan and I, but it was Reagan who promoted the idea of people helping each other as volunteers. It's volunteers who do most of the support work at the Dormitory and of course we couldn't operate without them."

The final question was from Luke's colleague. "Did you learn anything in India that helps you in your work?" It was, after all, Sunday morning.

"I still have an Indian guru," Mar said, "an old woman who lives in a remote village at the southern tip of India. She speaks hardly any English, but she was recommended to me because of her spirituality. She lives alone in what's really just a hut without even running water. When I was there I lived on vegetables cooked in water that was never very clean and I always had gastrointestinal problems. But I still use her as a guide in everything I do. I learned from her no one is an island any more, not people or countries. What happens in a remote village in India or Africa will ultimately have its effect on a city like New York or London or San Francisco. We've already seen that come true with the onset of this epidemic. I learned that spirituality has nothing to do with outward appearance. I think in the western hemisphere we think of spiritual people as sitting in white robes on top of some beautiful mountain in the Himalayas, because that's hard to get to, that's expensive, and we think that what's worth having costs a lot of money. But true spirituality maybe only exists in poverty and disease, because it's harder not to think about material things if you can hardly breath or if you have constant diarrhea. That's why I look for spiritual guidance to every client who comes to the Dormitory or the Factory. I don't think that AIDS was sent to teach us anything. But we can use it as an opportunity to learn spiritual values. What matters is love and service and forgiveness, not the frantic accumulation of material things. I had to be in the financial district the other day" – Mar happened to look straight into the camera just then and I felt the chill on the back of my neck, as if I'd finally recognized who'd been shadowing me all along – "and I felt the rage in the air. You see it on the freeway or in stores, or the way people treat each other lining up for popcorn at movie theaters. People are so full of rage at our society because it doesn't work any more, and they're helpless and trapped and don't know what to do."

The little face couldn't help looking pleased with itself, and the head lifted itself with pride as the camera drew back to observe him in profile under the closing credits. I felt pleased for Mar myself. It was a great performance. I thought: I'll use you as a guide, Mar. When I hear self-proclaimed goodness, I'll look for corruption. When someone invites trust, I'll look for deception. When I see displays of virtue, I'll wonder where the evil is hidden.

Chapter Twenty Eight

LUKE WAS STANDING outside his apartment house talking to a dark-haired older man who was cleaning out the inside of a yellow VW.

"Years ago he used to fuck me every Saturday morning while his laundry was in the wash cycle," Luke said as he opened his front door. "Then my friend Scoop, who used to live upstairs, told his lover who told that man's lover who forgave him as long as he promised never to do the laundry alone again. Oh well!" Luke made a nostalgic broken chuckling noise that was so effective it amazed me he hadn't incorporated it in his TV persona.

But I didn't laugh. I guess I was trying to cope with shock. Luke wore a short-sleeved knitted shirt with horizontal green and dark blue stripes. His forearms were covered with raised purple patches that looked as if they'd been tattooed to coordinate with the shirt.

I waited inside the door, forcing him to look at me, pleading silently for him to talk to me about what was happening to him.

He laughed and sighed and glanced down at his arms. "These are recent, just a few pretty gay lesions that know better than to come on my face and make me unemployable."

"They look like very expensive tattoos," I said wonderingly, "that someone made with a very rich and rare ink."

The feeling in my voice caught both of us unawares. He stole a look at me, then quickly looked away. "I'm going to have a little wine and Calistoga," he said. "You're welcome to join me in either or both of those things."

"Nothing," I said, and ended up waiting for him on the sofa as usual. He'd drawn the curtains over the doors into the garden against the mid-afternoon heat.

"We never expected a spring heat wave in San Francisco to last this long," Luke said, pretending it was the heat that was making him jumpy. He sat beside me balancing a tall glass and starting to push at the remote control for the TV.

"Tell me what's happening, Luke. Please."

He went on punching at the remote, then tossed it aside and turned and looked at me, but not for long. "I feel fine," he said. "There's no indication that the lesions are spreading internally. They're just a sign that my days are not unlimited. Judging from some of the other men I could still have two more years."

I wanted to believe him, but I didn't believe him, I was no expert.

"Does my mouth smell?" Luke asked suddenly. His eyes watered and he looked furtive until he controlled himself.

"Breathe on me," I said.

He leaned over quickly and panted into my face. Our eyes met for a second. I couldn't remember ever being so close to another man. I thought, detached: This is how it felt for Billy to be with his lovers. Luke's breath smelled slightly sour, maybe from the wine or yesterday's booze, but healthy.

"You smell fine," I said.

His face flushed a little, with relief or embarrassment, and he sat away. I knew he also enjoyed challenging me, forcing me to push against my limits. I knew he'd have liked to see me stymied. No way, if I could help it.

"I have thrush in my mouth and throat," he said. "We all have that, that's no big deal. I just don't want to smell. I went to the dentist yesterday to have two fillings done and I was afraid to ask him. He was wearing so many layers of protective masks he'd have trouble telling anyway." He tapped the bottom of his glass on the sofa arm. "I think I know what it's like to be passing on. I was lying there zonked on nitrous oxide and novocaine and the wine I'd drunk beforehand. After he did each filling he wiped it with some strong tasting stuff that was the same taste I remembered them using when I was a kid, and old memories were coming back while I was being tended to and having things done to me, and I knew that was exactly what it's like when you're in hospital at the end." He blinked and drank his drink, glancing quickly at me over the rim. "I panicked when I thought about it. This wasn't supposed to happen so soon."

"Do you think maybe it always happens too soon?" I asked, feeling completely inadequate. "I know you and your friends have a particular right to feel that, but I expect everybody feels it. I'm nearly 50 but I feel 30, and I still catch myself taking it for granted I have a lifetime ahead of me. It happened much too soon for Billy."

Luke banished the fed up expression he'd had, of someone who will cry if he's not careful. "What's happening with you?"

"I have a story for you," I said, but I was suddenly unconvinced myself, and not very interested for the moment. "I found out how Mar is creaming off money."

"Oh?" Luke said.

"Mar makes this big deal about giving all the money that's left over from the operation of the Factory to the Dormitory. I found out that almost all the $78,000 of private money the Dormitory got last year was well-publicized grants from foundations and private individuals. That money would have been too risky to tamper with; anybody would have been able to tell that Mar had left it off the balance sheet. But he doesn't give the money from the Factory directly to the Dormitory, although that's what his P.R. implies. He turns over the *investment proceeds* of the money, which means first of all a considerable time lag before the Dormitory sees anything."

Although I felt heartsick I still started enjoying what I was good at; setting up the facts of a situation, developing a logical argument, reaching a conclusion, which in this instance was fairly striking.

"The money is invested by Ferro Investments, Inc., which is a small financial planning corporation in Oakland. It's run in effect by one man, a Ralph Ferro. Over the last 18 months Ferro invested $140,000 of Factory money, all of it in high-risk long-term limited partnerships. That means that the investments aren't liquid – they have to be committed for several years and they produce little or no short-term income. Limited partnerships are also highly speculative, and their value could fluctuate with oil and gas prices. They're the kind of investments that people use as tax shelters, not to generate income. One of the partnerships has already gone bankrupt, wiping out Mar's investment, at least on paper. If Ferro had gone out of his way to lose Mar's money he couldn't have done a better job. The $140,000 has produced no more than $4,000 for the Dormitory so far."

I waited for an explosion from Luke, but it didn't come. "It sounds as if Mar chose the wrong investment adviser," he said. "But I never expected him to be a financial wizard. It sounds as if everybody's losing."

"I still need to find out who was involved in the limited partnerships where the money went," I continued impatiently. "My guess is that a lot of the money came back to Mar directly from Ferro or through a third party. At any rate, investments in limited partnerships produce much higher brokerage fees than regular investments. I'll bet Ferro split those fees with Mar."

"That's speculation," Luke said, something strained and disappointed in his face. "What Mar does with the Factory money is his business."

"What? He's getting tens of thousands of dollars from people who come to the Factory looking for a miracle, and doing this public relations promotion about giving it to the Dormitory when in fact the Dormitory is getting almost nothing."

"He doesn't have to give any money to the Dormitory."

"But he says he does, to make him look good. My guess is he started the Dormitory with peanuts, gambling that he'd be able to get massive amounts of city money once they saw what he was doing."

"You don't know that it was a deliberate ploy," Luke said. "Mar may have been swept along by the epidemic like everyone else. The investment broker may be defrauding Mar. The broker may just be incompetent."

"So what? The city is trusting hundreds of thousands of dollars a year to a man who is either a fraud or a fool. He could get a far better return if he invested the Factory money in a regular passbook savings account at Bank of America!"

I thought Luke would spring off the sofa, his body was so tense, his hands so tight. At other times when I'd argued with him about Marlin Golding he'd pretended to be mostly amused, never more than impatient. Now he looked worse than exasperated – trapped and ready to break. I felt him doing some internal equivalent of counting to ten. He got up and poured himself another, stronger drink. What he'd drunk so far hadn't been enough to sap his power, and I watched him visibly search for a reservoir of calm within himself to deal with me. He came back and sat close, facing me. He opened his mouth again and stuck out his tongue at me. At first I didn't understand what he was doing. He stuck out his tongue even further. In the center, like a black velvet jewel, there was a plump KS lesion. I felt full of pity for him, but angry, because I guessed he was about to use his sickness to manipulate me.

"We are in the middle of an epidemic that may end up killing over 50% of four or five generations of men," Luke said, as if he were making a last ditch stand to talk sense into a child. "The epidemic arrived quite suddenly at the beginning of the 80's. One year there were two or three whispers of a disaster that nobody understood. Two years later hundreds of men were dying inexplicably and two years later thousands were dying and now it's tens of thousands. Nobody was prepared for an epidemic. Nobody, neither institutions nor individuals, acted for the best. A few prophets saw the disaster that was coming, but we thought they had their own homophobic agendas and no one believed them soon enough. When the epidemic struck it felt as if it happened overnight. And ever since everybody has been trying to catch up. Resources and programs are swamped the moment they're implemented. But San Francisco, because it was a small centralized city where the people who were getting AIDS had a strong power base, did better than anywhere else. We raised money, we educated our own people to contain the epidemic, (even though the results in terms of people not coming down with the disease won't be seen for another ten years), and we cared for our own. We even tried to plan for the future so that the city wouldn't turn into a hellish charnel-house with thousands dying in the streets. I have to admit that we weren't perfect. The men and women who work in city government aren't real downtown hot shots with Ivy League educations who can charge $200 an hour for their services. Most of the people who handle AIDS at the Health Department and City Hall are second-rate and way in over their heads. Most of them never had a job before where they earned as much money as they earn now because of AIDS. And they waste money, because they're not particularly efficient or they don't know the going price for services. AIDS has been a boon to hundreds of social workers and counselors in this city who otherwise could never have hoped to find employment, to whom the idea of having to work hard in the financial district seemed like a fate worse than death. The minute there's a cure for AIDS the only living they'll have left is to organize seminars on bridging the transition from death back to life. There's been enough AIDS money to take care of more than a few cheap hustlers with a finger in every pie. What we have in San Francisco is thousands of ordinary people working in the AIDS industry who maybe start out idealistic and burning with love or who maybe just jump at the opportunity to earn a living. Either way they generally burn out real soon, but they stay on anyway because it's the best living that's available to them and on balance they do an adequate job."

Luke had kept me from interrupting him. "In that context," he said, "I don't see what Mar is doing that's so terrible. He's providing a much-needed service. He may or may not be skimming off money from the Factory, but the Factory is his own private operation. He may run the Dormitory inefficiently or even pocket a percentage, and the city officials who examine his books may not really know what to look for. But we don't have the time or the resources to be perfect. If there wasn't the Dormitory there'd be nowhere else for most of the homeless people with AIDS to go. That's the bottom line."

I started to speak but Luke shrugged me off again. "There's one more thing. Federal and local government are looking for any excuse to reduce funding for AIDS programs."

"I don't –"

"Let's not even discuss why they ignored AIDS for so many years. Let's just say they were born with a disease like color blindness; they lack emotional empathy unless it suits their ambitions. All these people need is an AIDS money scandal in San Francisco and they'll argue that the money they've already committed is more than enough if only it wasn't wasted."

I was perversely glad that Luke had something he cared about enough to be so angry and eloquent. But his urgency rekindled mine. "You're saying hands off AIDS programs until the epidemic is under control. You're saying get involved with AIDS and you get a free ride whatever sins you commit."

"Maybe that is what I'm saying. Maybe one day there'll be time again to discuss fine points of ethics."

"What you do during the epidemic will determine what you do in peacetime – I mean when AIDS is gone. You'll become what you do now. This city will be filled with a crowd that's dependent for a living on the cronies they made deals with during AIDS."

Luke shrugged.

"What does Marlin Golding have on you, Luke?"

He stared at me, then sighed and threw up his hands in real or faked exasperation.

"A story is a story," I said, "whether it's AIDS or something else. We already know about the researchers cutting each other's throats to get the Nobel, the doctors who don't want to treat AIDS patients, the burnout and drug abuse among health care workers who deal with AIDS. One juicy scandal isn't going to bring down the AIDS industry. The government probably assumes it's inefficient and corrupt. They're used to it. Why are you protecting Mar?"

"There's nothing to protect him from except your speculation," Luke cried. "There is no story!"

"I know he killed Billy or arranged to have him killed. Those people reek of guilt. I know they set me up with Valerie. I know they were going to accuse me of raping her to discredit me."

"Maybe Valerie thinks you did rape her," Luke said.

"Have you been talking to her?" He shook his head. "They set me up. She tried to provoke me into beating her up. She left cuts and scratches on my body to make it look as if she'd tried to fight me. She didn't want me to use a rubber. She tried to take the rubber afterwards. She didn't want me to call a taxi from her apartment because it would look as if we'd parted friends. Why did you offer to lie for me, Luke? Why did you tell me to say I'd been with you?"

Luke shook his head. I thought he was about to put his hands over his ears.

"So that if it got as far as the police and I did choose to say I'd been with you you could deny it? Did they tell you to make that offer to me?" Luke's eyes were filling. "You seem to know every one of them. Would you have lied for them?"

"I did a story on them. I told you everybody knows

everybody else in San Francisco."

"The man who first told me about Mar and the Factory is dead as well now," I said. "He supposedly killed himself, although he'd arranged to die with his friends beside him when he chose to go. Jerry died shortly after I told you about him. Why were you so ready to take a cameraman down to the Dormitory when I told you about the maze? Because it was easy to warn Mar in advance?"

Luke was shrinking, looking battered and tired. I realized he was sick, and realized that was something I hadn't wanted to admit, whatever evidence of it I saw.

"Why would Mar have Billy killed?" he asked. "You've never been able to explain that."

"Because he found out what I've been finding out."

"It isn't worth murdering for."

"I think to Mar it is. It's Mar's survival we're talking about, in the manner he's grown accustomed to. But probably there's more. Something that is worth murdering for. Whatever they searched Billy's apartment for and found or didn't find."

Luke stood up and hesitated over whether to head for the nearly empty wine bottle. "I'm going to take a nap. You're welcome to stay. You can sit in the garden if you like." I shook my head.

Luke chose to make himself another drink, pottering around the bottles with his back to me. "This is what I think. They'll never find out who killed Billy. Maybe it was some drug or sex scene that went too far. But Mar had nothing to do with it. And if that's the case, none of the rest of this stuff is really any of your business. You're not interested in AIDS or shelters for homeless PWA's or who's exploiting who. If the police found Billy's killer tomorrow you'd lose all interest in Mar and you'd leave San Francisco. Wouldn't you?"

I didn't like Luke's scenario. It implied rejection of all I had left that concerned or involved me. It implied rejection of him.

Luke took a good swallow of his drink. "What I also see is terrible paranoia. You're running after your own tail and blaming other people. I think you people call it a dry drunk. I don't think I'll ever stop drinking. It doesn't look like much fun."

I gazed at him. I tried to say with my eyes: I'm certainly

somewhat crazy, I think I know why you're trying to drive me away, you won't stop me caring about you.

"I'm going to take my nap," Luke said.

I wanted to say something about him being sick, but I couldn't think of what to say. When I let myself out it seemed as if our friendship had ended.

As I walked home I thought that I had almost nothing now, no more leads, no friends after these weeks in San Francisco, nothing more to say to Luke that he wouldn't cut short. In desperation I pulled one remembered name out of the waste.

"I remember you very well," Imogen Brown said. "Well, Frank left us a week ago. My boy is gone."

Of course. "I'm very sorry," I said.

"So am I," Imogen said. "But at least he isn't in pain any more. I don't think I could have stood it if he'd had to suffer any more pain. Would you like to come to dinner?"

Chapter Twenty Nine

IMOGEN LIVED A few blocks away, on a steep tree-lined street I'd often climbed as I ran towards Golden Gate Park. Wild flowers crowded into a long window box over the entrance to the ground floor garage of the red brick house. A purple-flowered vine whose name I didn't know glowed in the fog and climbed the front walls almost to the eaves, invading the windows on its way.

There were broad white steps leading from a wrought iron gate to the heavy wooden door. My knock was answered by a very tall, very thin man, about ten years older than me, with short salt-and-pepper hair and a snow-white moustache. He looked friendly but under tight control.

"I'm Ed," he said, "Frank's oldest brother."

"We have something in common," I said.

He led me into a high-ceilinged intricately lit living room more spacious than I'd expected from the house's narrow exterior. A wood fire hissed and chattered its self-created drama, enriching the dark blue of the carpet and the burgundy upholstery. Away at the end of the room, behind a curved archway, Imogen in a black dress was lighting tall white candles on a great circular glass dining table. I thought: I suppose she inherited money or married it or both. I don't expect she worked for it. But thank God there's comfort and protection somewhere.

"Hello," Imogen called sadly and inched towards me pushing one side of her body at a time, will overcoming frailty. "I'm so glad you could come tonight." I noticed as she got near that her black dress was faded and mended. "I hope you don't mind a big fire in the middle of a heat wave. Ed says it's silly but this house gets *chilly* at night and it looks cheerful. I sorely need some cheering up."

She looked up at me with the same quizzical humorous resigned expression, her eyelids red.

"You have beautiful blue eyes," I said. "Periwinkle they'd call them in a kid's story. I remembered them."

Imogen stared at me as if she was reading my lips or translating what she'd heard. After a delay she lifted both hands to her temples. "Oh no!" she said. "Frank always said I had periwinkle eyes. I think I'm going to cry. No I'm not going to cry. I promised Ed I wouldn't cry this evening."

"I'm fixing Brandy Alexanders," Ed said. "It's a family tradition when I'm in town."

"Not for me," I said. "I'll have some fruit juice."

"Are you sure?" Ed asked. "How about scotch? I brought Mother a bottle of very good scotch and if we don't drink it Mother will only drink it by herself and make a lot of inappropriate phone calls to her grandchildren."

"Don't disgrace me, Ed," Imogen cried in a simulated fury. "I'm tired of you disgracing me in front of family and friends." She appealed to me. "Once I was talking on the telephone to one of my grandsons and I had a slight cold. And Victor I think it was said afterwards to his mother, 'Grandma sounded drunk.' Nobody in the family has ever let me forget it, especially Ed. I'd have thought after all these years of living I'd have earned some respect from my children, wouldn't you?"

I sank into an armchair so gratefully that I recognized how tired I was and starved for ordinary company. While Ed fetched the drinks Imogen sat opposite me, smoothing the hem of her dress, I think to comfort herself, while she thought of ways to interest me.

"My son Ed builds bridges in Portland," she said. "He was a pilot in the Korean war. His wife Carol is my favorite person in the whole world except for Frank, although I know I'm not supposed to have favorites. She's given me seven grandchildren, one of whom died, and two greatgrandchildren so far."

"Stop bragging, Mother," Ed said. Imogen got up as soon as he settled on the sofa next to my armchair.

"I'll leave you to get acquainted," she said. "Dinner will only be a few minutes." She remained, murmuring to herself, for a few moments longer, then began to propel herself towards the kitchen.

"Thank you for coming," Ed said warily. "If you hadn't come tonight she'd have gone to bed early without eating and cried herself to sleep. Frank was her favorite. She saw more of him because he was the only one of us who stayed in the city. The last 18 months while he was sick her whole life was taken up with taking care of him."

"I only met him once," I said, "and by then he was very sick indeed. It was Imogen I talked to. Frank and I never even said hello."

Ed brushed that aside. "Mother said they met you at the Healing Factory," he said, putting the name in quotation marks. There was a shadow still in his voice and face. "Are they friends of yours?"

"No," I said. "They very much are not friends of mine."

"Thank God," Ed said, relaxing visibly. Somehow I knew I'd moved closer to finding a means of destroying Mar.

On her sparkling table with heavy silver and immaculate white linen napkins, Imogen served a small pot roast.

"For years after the children left I had trouble cutting my cooking down to the proper amounts," she said. "I always made far too much of everything."

I picked up a fork, then noticed that Imogen and Ed had bowed their heads.

"For these oh Lord thy bountiful gifts we thank thee," Imogen murmured. "*Now* you can start," she said to me with mock severity.

The roast was overdone and the vegetables cooked almost to a watery puree. It occurred to me that this was the kind of food you learned to cook to meet the demands of generations of children.

"I'd like to propose one last toast to my son," Imogen said after Ed poured the wine. I raised my glass of juice. "To Frank, wherever that boy is now. I miss him so much, and I know I'll miss him until the day I die."

She chewed a very small forkful, then pointed to the rows of framed photographs on a sideboard. "That's Frank," she said. "I know you wouldn't recognize him because you only saw him at the end, but that's Frank the way he used to be."

Children and men and women of all ages, alone and in couples and in family groups, crowded the sideboard in snapshots and idealized studio portraits. I only recognized Frank because Imogen pointed at him and the photograph was the largest, and at the front. I didn't like it; it was an attempt to make a matinee idol of an ordinary man who couldn't help looking hard and sly. There was a smaller picture of Ed and his wife next to it. Both of them looked as if they wanted to get it over with as fast as possible.

"I can't stop asking myself *why*," Imogen said. "I know Ed doesn't want me to talk about it in front of you but I can't *help* it. Why did Frank have to die? Why do all these men I keep reading about in the newspapers have to die? And children, who'll never get a chance to live? It just doesn't make any sense. There are members of my own family I think I'll have difficulty ever speaking to again. Francine made the mistake of telling Anne-Marie – I *knew* she shouldn't have done that – and Anne-Marie told Sidney, which was asking for trouble, and Sidney wrote me a disgraceful cold awful letter saying he hoped God would forgive Frank. *I* will never forgive *Sidney*. AIDS is nothing to be proud of, but it's certainly nothing to be ashamed of. How could anyone possibly be ashamed of having a deadly disease?"

Ed watched his mother with a kind of subdued misery. He'd closed down again over some unspoken issue.

"I don't think I can bear to go to Ed and Carol's for Christmas this year if Sidney is going to be there," Imogen said. "I think Carol had better drop a tactful hint that Sidney had better find some other way of celebrating this Christmas."

Ed drank his wine, eyes downcast.

"It just isn't fair," Imogen said, appealing to me. "I know you both probably think I should keep quiet, but I don't want to keep quiet. Frank didn't deserve to die, and he didn't deserve to go through all that suffering. He was a gift to the world. Oh, he tormented me and teased me even more than Ed does, but he was a joy and he was *fun*. 'Mother,' he said, 'the virus will not continue to live in my body because I'll give it such a hard time even the AIDS virus will move someplace else.'" Imogen chuckled sadly. "And I believed him. Until the very last day I believed a miracle would happen and he'd be spared. The priests at the church *encouraged* me to believe that. But I suppose miracles don't happen anymore, although I know I'm not supposed to say that either. And now I'll stop. I *will* stop talking about it. I have no right to inflict my unhappiness on you. Ed, tell our guest about some of your adventures in the navy." Then she stamped her fist on the table. "But Ed won't even let me into Frank's apartment. He says it would bring back too many memories. But I *want* as many memories as I can hold on to. I want to sort through Frank's things myself and be as close to him as I can get. They're all I have left of him."

Ed offered to walk home with me.

"I thought I didn't know the name of that vine," I said outside the house. "It's bougainvillea. I used to visit houses where they grew bougainvillea. I used to hope my life would have some grace and order in it. I've lost a lot of memories. I might just as well have chopped them out of my brain."

Ed said nothing. I'm not sure he'd even listened to me.

I made a guess. "Had you known your brother was gay?"

"No," he said with great relief, and once he started to talk it all came tumbling out compulsively. "Mother knew all along it was AIDS, but she played tricks with us. She didn't tell us how ill he really was until the very end, and he had so many diseases that go along with AIDS that she never had to mention the primary cause. It was pneumonia, or intestinal cancer that he was getting radiation for. I think she even wanted AIDS left off the death certificate, but they wanted to do an autopsy for research purposes and they had to say why. I'd arrived by then and that was the first time I heard it mentioned. I was stunned, but it all suddenly made sense. But Mother and I can't talk about what it means that Frank died of AIDS. We can't say 'gay.' It's sitting there between us, but we talk around it."

I told him about my gay brother Billy.

"I can't forgive Frank for lying to us for so many years," Ed said. "He built a whole double life to stop us knowing who he really was. One Christmas he even brought home a young woman he said he was engaged to. I wonder if that wasn't a pretense, if they hadn't made some arrangement."

170

"Maybe not," I said. "Maybe he was trying to be somebody he wasn't."

"Why?" Ed said. "We were family for over 50 years. Didn't he know how deeply I felt about that? Didn't he trust me?"

"Sidney is family," I reminded him with some reluctance.

"We were brothers," Ed said impatiently. "I had to go to Frank's apartment to pick up a dark suit to bury him in. I took one look and barred Imogen from ever going there. She said she wanted to see it because she'd never been there after Frank moved in. He always told her he preferred coming to her house for home cooking. Isn't that strange, what families tolerate? Mother and Frank lived within a mile of each other for 20 years and she never saw his apartment. There was a room in his apartment that looked like a torture chamber. There were drugs that must have been worth a fortune that I wrapped up and threw in the garbage. There was an apron I thought I'd take back to Mother and fortunately I opened it up and there was a picture of a mouth with a moustache sucking on a penis. I thought I'd seen everything in the navy. Men would come to me for advice and mention things I'd never thought existed. But this is the most shocking thing that ever happened to me. Carol is the only woman I've ever been to bed with. Once or twice I went to whorehouses overseas with my friends to see what they were like but I never used any of the women. Frank's life bewilders and saddens me, but what hurts me most is that he lived a lie and he didn't trust me enough to tell me who he was."

I thought I'd offer a little perspective. "I was married once for less than two years and I was unfaithful to her from the second week," I said. "In the 20 years since then I've nearly always paid for the women I went to bed with."

Ed stopped and met my eyes. After a moment he nodded and his face relaxed. We continued walking down Duboce. The park was deserted in the fog except for the dog walkers and a woman jogging in several layers of sweats. Behind the houses the downtown lights fired the fog with all the empty promises of a once-a-year fairground.

"Frank's finances are in chaos," Ed said. "They repossessed his car and he was about to lose the apartment. He owed about $60,000 and he had almost no assets. A week before he died, when he was almost too weak to move, he wrote a check for $5,000 to Marlin Golding."

At last. I felt the surge.

"The check was returned for insufficient funds. I hardly recognized the handwriting and I think someone may have forged his signature. Three weeks before that he wrote Golding another check for $5,000 and that one cleared. I'm not sure the handwriting on that one is Frank's either. The money was Mother's. She gave it to Frank to keep his creditors at bay while he died in peace. Instead it went to some charlatan. Carol and I will have to get the money together and give it back to Mother. All she has left is the house. We keep trying to persuade her to sell it but she doesn't want to and we don't really want her to. We don't want that part of our lives to end. Frank can't have known what he was doing if he wrote those checks. What kind of people would steal from a man in the last few days of a terrible disease?"

"The people who murdered my brother," I said. I glanced at Ed, and saw no shadow of surprise or disbelief in his face. "Are you willing to talk to the police and the newspapers?" I asked.

"I don't know," he said. "I think so, if you think it's necessary."

"First let's try and get the money back. This is what you do." Since I stopped practicing law I'd become less likely to recommend that people hire attorneys. "Write Mar a letter tomorrow, certified mail, return receipt requested. Say it's come to your notice that he received $5,000 from your brother shortly before he died and even tried to cash another check for $5,000 as Frank was dying. Say you're certain Mar wouldn't have accepted the money if he'd known that Frank was deeply in debt and so sick that he couldn't possibly have known what he was doing, since that money belonged to his creditors. Say you're certain Mar will return the money now that he knows the circumstances, and you'll expect a certified check within five days, and hope it won't be necessary for you to take further action. Don't say what the further action might be. Mar's imagination may be more powerful than anything you can threaten. There are going to be a lot more accusations, and Mar may think giving the money back to you would be a good public relations move. If you do get your money we can still use it against Mar that he ever took it in the first place. I can probably find other families he's taken from in similar circumstances. I thought he was too smart to be so greedy."

"May I ask you a question?" Ed said outside my door. "Are you gay?"

"No," I said, irritated that once you were connected with it you became subject to scrutiny.

"I went for a walk in the Castro yesterday," Ed said. "There were couples holding hands and walking with their arms around each other. I think they must be especially open and loving."

"That's sentimental, Ed," I said. "They're no more open or loving than anyone else."

Chapter Thirty

I WANTED TO make one more quick move before I took my accusations to City Hall.

Mar was not listed in the San Francisco telephone directory but there were seven other Goldings listed. I tried the men first, but they all expressed surprise when I suggested they might have an apartment vacant.

It was a Ruby Golding who I guessed must be Mar's mother. Things fell my way with ridiculous ease. "We'll have a vacant apartment in three weeks," she said. "The tenant doesn't like me going in there when he's at work, but you can look at this one. The layout is the same." Her voice was ingratiating and even, nothing to suggest where Mar got his on-and-off accent.

The apartment building comprised four featureless grey stories northeast of the park. The northern side of the street was lined with similar middle income buildings packed with rooms. The southern side was in the middle of redevelopment, and the house opposite the Goldings' building had ben built to fit between two houses that were now torn down. It looked incongrously narrow, like the image on a wide screen movie squeezed to fit TV.

I rang the bell with "Manager" against it. "Yoo-hoo," a voice called from outside. Ruby Golding was wiping her hands on a floral apron at the bottom of the steps down to the basement. I greeted her with frank friendly warmth, having no intention other than to exploit her.

"This is what the upstairs is like, except that the apartment you're interested in was painted more recently," she said, holding her door for me, eager-to-please, a little apologetic, trying to be businesslike.

The door opened directly into a medium-sized low-ceilinged living room where a man sat playing with a poker at the cinders in a grate. He wore greasy old black trousers and a collarless shirt worn through at the elbows. He didn't look up.

"There are no fireplaces in the upstairs apartments," Ruby said. She was white haired and her body had spread comfortably. "How did you hear about us? Usually I advertise if an apartment is going to be vacant and the other tenants don't know anyone who's looking."

"I'm a friend of Mar's," I said. The man looked up, his eyes expressionless, his eyebrows arching with arrogance that seemed ridiculously inappropriate. He cleared his throat to make some point and went back to exploring the cinders.

"I don't see much of my son these days, except in the papers," Ruby said. "How is Marlin?"

"Thriving," I said. "Is this the apartment where he grew up?"

"Marlin and his sister," Ruby said, still a little apologetic.

The living room carried no traces of the children who'd lived there, maybe because it had been cleared to make more room for the needs of a building full of tenants: parcels and large envelopes Ruby had taken in, lamps and tables stranded awaiting repair, a rug Ruby was in the middle of cleaning.

"Let me show you the other rooms," she said.

The bathroom/toilet was barely big enough to turn around in. The kitchen was larger; they could have squeezed in a dining table big enough for four. The bedroom was a large closet, a dark smothering space past a doorless archway in the living room. Next to the row of coats and dresses pressed against the bed that nearly filled the alcove there was a dresser with letters and notes on the top. But Ruby had preceded me into the room. There was no space left to follow her. She motioned me back out of the archway and crossed over to the window which faced the basement steps and a cement wall, with light showing through the railings at the top. She spread her arms spaciously. "Your apartment would have a clear view facing south," she said.

The telephone rang. Ruby answered it, picking up in the middle of a tight conversation about some service that hadn't been performed to a tenant's satisfaction. I slipped through the archway. As I passed through I felt the man look up again. I stepped back against the bed out of his view. I calculated that he could see the side and top of the dresser. I craned to see the return addresses on the letters, reaching out a finger to move them into the light from the living room. Ruby hung up. One of the envelopes, with photographs sticking out of the top, had a handwritten return address in Oakland. I pulled it towards me, certain that Golding could see my hand, and dropped it in my jacket pocket as Ruby appeared in the archway. Blood was having a hard time pushing through my head.

"I was looking at the walls," I said, "to see if there was any dampness."

"There's no dampness upstairs," Ruby said coldly.

When we went back in the living room the man was watching me.

I began talking too quickly. "I'm not sure. It's a trade-off. I'm not sure if I'd rather pay more money for more space. How soon do you need to know?"

As I left Ruby was heading back to the telephone. I fled the street they lived on, sweating, cutting a block north and then two blocks east out of my way. I wasn't cut out to be a thief.

The photographs were of Ruby's grandchildren. The letter was from Mar's sister Sylvia, who was married to Ralph Ferro.

Chapter Thirty One

WHEN I GOT home that day the thick glass panel that made up most of my front door had been destroyed – hacked away so that the wooden frame was empty except for triangles of glass in the upper corners. A torn strip of the lace cloth that had been tacked to the inside of the door still clung to one side of the frame; the rest lay under shards of thick glass rippled at the edges. On top of the mess the mailman had tossed that day's mail, scattered junk mail addressed to William Phillips or Current Resident. I remembered the opened mail I found thrown on the same floor the night I arrived at the apartment from Minneapolis.

A kid on a skateboard glanced up at me, grinning curiously as he flowed by. Otherwise the business of the street went on uninterrupted. I felt almost nothing, the beginning of a sinking feeling, while I did what had to be done. I stepped inside through the empty frame and went upstairs. There were no obvious signs that anyone had entered the apartment. I carried down the door I'd taken off its hinges, then I found masking tape to crisscross over the outside of the empty frame as a keep out warning. As I was cutting it the next front door opened and the abused young woman flounced out, staring straight ahead.

"Did you see who did this?" I asked her.

Her eyes flicked towards me. She locked the door behind her and took off. "I saw nobody do nothing," she called over her shoulder.

The spare door leaning against the inside of the front door completely covered the empty panel except for the space at the bottom where I had to tilt it to keep it from falling over. I ran tape over that space to discourage Tom from getting out, if he was still here. I went upstairs and called the landlord, who promised to have a carpenter there before the end of the day. Then I started looking for the cat. First in the likely places - his hideaway at the back of the bookcase, behind the refrigerator, at the back of the closet where I'd stacked the blinds I'd taken down. Then systematically, starting at the southern end of the apartment and checking each room fully before I moved on. Periodically I'd look over the banisters to make sure he wasn't retreating before me, because he generally anticipated the worst and hated me to search for him. Drenched with sweat, I was finally certain that the cat was gone.

I called Luke at home because I thought he might not have left for the station. I left a message on his machine. Then I called the newsroom and they told me he was unavailable. I got angry at him when I started listing the alternative candidates he'd find to blame for breaking the door: the landlord, or the neighbors, getting revenge because I hadn't gone along with the plan to get the house repaired at the utility's expense. I knew that I'd been punished for digging into Mar's affairs and warned against digging any further.

So far in San Francisco I'd tried to forget the trickles of fear. Maybe in order to keep going I hadn't thought through the implications of what I was involved in. Maybe Luke had convinced me his version was true but I couldn't admit it because then I'd never be able to repay my debt to Billy. Maybe it hadn't sunk in that I was dealing with murder, or that Billy was really dead. That afternoon it finally made sense to me to believe that my life was in danger, and I was scared and trapped. I'd have fled the apartment and checked into a motel but I was waiting for a call from some stranger who'd found Tom. I needed to believe there was a good chance that would happen. It made perfect sense to me to jeopardize my life for an animal that had brought me comfort and warmth and taught me to honor its particular vision of the world we shared.

The workman hadn't come by three o'clock. I called the landlord to find out what was happening and I ordered him to tell the carpenter to bring a burglar alarm. When he began to argue I threatened to turn him in to City Hall and the IRS for under-reporting his income.

I was accustomed to being one of the last to know what I was feeling. That afternoon I felt stabs of fear and anger, but still mostly I watched fear and anger build inside me as I struggled to move my body through the rest of the day. I ate an apple and some soup. I called Luke again and still got his machine. I knew he'd dismiss the news about the investment manager being part of Mar's family – so what? – but I didn't think he could dismiss Mar stealing from patients about to die. I'd tell him that if he didn't want the story I'd give it to the other networks. But I began to feel I'd failed: I still hadn't proved that Mar and his friends had killed Billy, or even demonstrated that they'd been involved. This is the scenario I created in my head: Luke interviewed three or four families of dying patients from whom Mar had taken money; the city announced that it was cancelling its contract with Mar and funding Catholic Social Services or the Episcopal Sanctuary to open a shelter that provided identical services to the same population. Mar had to close the Dormitory and attendance at the Factory fell off after the scandal; Mar, ever adaptable and resourceful, moved on, perhaps to another city where AIDS was only beginning to reach epidemic level; he took with him all hope of ever finding out the truth about Billy's death.

Then I lived this scene: I could disappear from the house in Minneapolis for two or three days without anyone realizing I'd been gone; I followed Mar to his next city, taking a roundabout route on different airlines, paying cash for each stage of the journey, wearing a simple disguise; I found where he'd set up his new enterprise and waited for him to leave at night and murdered him on a dark street, stabbing him in the heart with a kitchen knife I'd bought between planes in a big busy store in some distant city. Mar would be easy to kill. As I pictured the irrevocable moment when I turned the knife in his heart and I joined the large community of killers that roam the earth, his face shifted to become the face of the partner who'd fired me, then the face of a woman who'd turned me down long years ago; I admitted to myself for the first time in my life how badly I'd wanted her.

A carpenter came at four o'clock and told me all he had time to do that day was take some measurements and nail boards across the inside of the door and fix up a makeshift alarm that might or might not go off if somebody tried to come in the front door again. I hardly paid attention to him, although I still hovered at the top of the stairs in case Tom crept out of some hiding place I hadn't found and ran out the front door.

I wondered if taking four or five shorter plane trips wouldn't increase the danger of my being noticed and remembered.

I don't know when I switched back to a cloudy uneasy kind of reality, or why; maybe I was genetically programmed not to go mad. I wouldn't kill Mar or anyone else, and that seemed to me a failure. Because then the only choice left me was to coexist with Mar and his kind; if I couldn't avoid clashing with them I was doomed to be the victim, because unlike them I had scruples, because there were things I wouldn't do, maybe because there were risks I wouldn't take with my own life, even to avenge a brother's murder.

The phone never rang all day. I talked to it, begging it to ring, even if it turned out to be the landlord calling to find out if the door had been fixed. I called Luke at the apartment again and still got his machine. I called him again at the studio and they said he was unavailable. But he wasn't on the early evening news. I lay on the sofa in a fever while the heat made unsettling vertical shifts in the gardens below and as I reviewed my failures it grew dark without my noticing. After dark I called Luke again and still got his machine. Then as I went to the bathroom I noticed a familiar light at the other end of the apartment. I thought: They've come back.

As I headed towards the room facing the street I saw that the red candle was burning in the darkened second story of the newly built house opposite. The light slid out, then on again, as someone passed in front of it. I turned on the front room light and stood in the window and made a Fuck You sign and held it. Then I turned out the light. The candle burned on. As long as I watched there were no further signs of movement in the room.

Much later it occurred to me that Luke knew the secret of Billy's murder and he would tell me the truth if I drank with him. I knew how angry he was at me for sitting judging him while he drank, how he kept drinking so that he could swallow his anger at me. It made sense that if I took him a couple of bottles of good wine and drank them with him he'd stop being angry at me. I was sure that when Luke and I had shared a few drinks Luke would tell me all he really knew about Mar, and we'd plan what we could do together to make sure Mar got what he deserved. Later on Luke would probably give me a few pointers on what really went through your head when you were young and about to die. I couldn't wait for the eleven o'clock news to see what story Luke had been covering so that I'd have an excuse to call him again and suggest going round. I hoped the liquor stores would still be open. I expected that very soon now I'd destroy myself.

At the same time, as I waited, I began to be filled with a larger dread that seemed to have nothing to do with my own sickness, as if I could draw accurate conclusions from the fragments of information that had been reaching me throughout the day from the world beyond my head.

"As happens so often in San Francisco," the co-anchor said, "AIDS stories top tonight's news. There is some very good news for AIDS victims, and there is some very bad news for all of us at Channel 7.

"*Science* magazine will report next week the success of preliminary trials of an AIDS treatment developed by Nobel Prize winning British scientist Dr. Burnett McBride. The treatment is a combination of genetically engineered virus fighters and drugs that boost the immune system. None of the 20 AIDS patients tested with the drugs over nine months have developed further opportunistic infections. McBride says he believes the treatment will prevent the disease developing in victims who have already been infected with HIV but show no signs of illness.

"The British press is predicting tonight that McBride's discovery virtually assures him of another Nobel Prize. We'll have more on the breakthrough from our medical correspondent later in this newscast and also responses from Bay Area AIDS patients and workers."

Pause. Switch to gravity. "Tonight's very serious and sadly ironic news is that Channel 7 reporter Luke Carroll is fighting for his life tonight at Davies Medical Center. Luke's colleague Barbara Zahn is at the hospital now."

Cut to Barbara in a corridor outside intensive care. She glances guardedly sideways as she talks in low tones into the microphone. "Luke was admitted to intensive care late this afternoon suffering from the AIDS-related pneumonia PCP. A doctor I spoke to ten minutes ago said his condition is quote extremely grave unquote. I've also learned that Luke's family has been contacted and is flying in. Although most HIV patients survive the first attack of PCP, Luke may have a harder time fighting back because he has been living with other AIDS diseases for many months. I'm Barbara Zahn, reporting from Davies Medical Center."

Cut to anchor. "Luke was diagnosed with Kaposi's Sarcoma skin cancer over a year ago. We learned today that his KS spread rapidly during the last few weeks, but he kept his worsening condition secret, wanting to continue working as long as possible. The hospital has requested that viewers do not telephone, so that lines can be kept open to provide vital services for other patients."

Chapter Thirty Two

I SUPPOSE THE fog's cold needles pricked away my fever as I tore up the hill to that concrete block of a hospital.

Intensive Care belied its name if you expected crisis and tension. One nurse was on duty at her station in a calm corridor. Machines monitored and regulated the tortured bodies.

"Are you family?" she asked with a certain genuine concern when I spoke Luke's name.

"Yes," I said.

She looked grim. "He's very peaceful."

Luke's colleague had gone home, I supposed to be replaced when it came time to get material for the morning news. There were no traces of the carnival that came later: the banks of flowers and food, the fans acting entitled, the "political activists" who'd criticized the political correctness of every story Luke did and now pontificated for the cameras on his significance in the gay history of the city. The brief appearances of the Mayor and various supervisors were duly taped.

That night the muscles had already shrunk in Luke's body. The wall behind his bed in the small warm room was stacked with machines, few of which seemed to be in use. Luke slept soundly, bare chested and propped against pillows, oxygen prongs in his nose, a trac tube taped securely to his neck and chest but nicely avoiding the purple lesions, an IV in each arm, the coil of a penile catheter sticking out under the sheet.

I sat on the bed and looked into his unguarded face. He had faded as if bleach had stripped the color from his face and the texture from his hair. I was seized with despair and rage so strong that my body started to tremble. I wanted to shake him back to consciousness. I thought: You motherfucker, don't take the easy way out of a fight with me. I began to cry.

Luke's shoulders jerked and he frowned slightly, then he smiled at some deep warm memory.

I prayed, clear headed: *Let Luke live and I'll never ask for anything again. Don't punish me any more for being afraid of living. Let Luke live and I'll spend the rest of my life fighting the epidemic. I'll never drink again. Let Luke live and I'll thank you for whatever happens to me from now until I die. Let Luke live and I won't seek revenge on Mar.* Then it occurred to me that bargaining might not be the best way to get what I wanted, so I made some unconditional promises, and waited, fully expecting a miracle.

Later in the morning, when people started arriving, I told a nurse as I slipped away that Luke's bedclothes needed changing.

"There's shit in the bed," I said, to demonstrate urgency.

"He's incontinent of stool," he corrected me calmly.

Some days I went to the hospital two or three times, but it became hard to get near him and I felt as if I had low priority. His parents looked bewildered. I avoided talking to them because even from a distance I felt proprietorial, as if no one from outside the city could understand the significance of what was happening to Luke.

As it became clear that Luke was going to die, I think choosing to inch towards death at that particular time because what had he left now that he craved?, I got to grieve for Billy as I grieved for Luke. Grief softened me and grief hardened me, because as I lived through the loss of what I loved and had loved I learned the value of hatred. I bought a typewriter and typed a balance sheet with all the evidence I had against Mar, and all the arguments I could think of against the evidence. Every day I revised it, honed it and perfected it, objectively assessing the weight of the evidence I intended to use to destroy the thing I hated. It became clear to me that I only had enough to destroy his game, to take away his income and his power, though I knew he'd fight for them to the bitter end. I wondered what I was going to do about that. Because evidence wasn't everything. I knew Mar had killed Billy, or I was sure he'd killed him, or I was

90% certain. Luke might have said to me – lying to me, but if I waited for friends who'd never betray me I'd be lonely for the rest of my life – "It could just as well be your imagination, your paranoia, your blaming yourself for your addicted past by blaming people who are druggies now." But I didn't need certainty any more. From now on I'd act on what I believed.

One afternoon I went to the hospital and found Mar and Wink in the corridor. Mar was dressed in a brocade tunic that looked something like Hollywood's idea of some Eastern burial robe. As I turned into the corridor he was about to lay his hands on Luke's mother's temples in an awful travesty of some profound healing moment as she gazed at him with startled eyes. Something snapped in me and I started running towards them.

"Take your hands off her you obscene piece of shit," I shouted as I reached them and grabbed Mar and pulled him away and pushed him along the corridor towards the elevator. He almost flew away from me as I whirled to meet Wink's attack. Wink ignored me, moving towards his lover to protect him as nurses came running, his hands raised so that the big muscles were flexed. But they weren't built for use. He glanced at me helplessly as he edged around me sideways then ran to pick up Mar, who'd fallen on one knee. The elevator doors opened and Wink lifted Mar inside. I watched, then ran towards them, but the doors closed.

When I reached the parking lot, baking in the dry burning air. Mar was starting up a blue Volvo and Wink was getting into a red Pontiac Firebird. I ran over and banged on the roof of the Volvo as it backed away, then I yelled as I pulled back my hand, which hurt so badly that I thought the scorching metal had torn my skin off. I ran after the Volvo and only just managed to skim the side as Mar sped away. I turned to block Wink. He waited behind the Firebird's wheel. Mar was already turning onto Castro. I could hardly see Wink's face in the glare. I tried to turn him into a villain but it was too hard. I shrugged and stepped aside and let him go in search of his lover. Some kinds of love I didn't understand.

It had happened so quickly that when I woke up later from an exhausted nap, stale and heavy and bitter, I might have thought I'd hallucinated it. But my hand still stung.

One morning at two o'clock when I couldn't sleep I went up to the hospital and watched from the doorway as a large black woman in a lime green dress cradled Luke's head and shoulders as spiking fevers erupted through his body, which was packed in ice. Steam rose from his skin.

She looked up and our eyes met. Two large tears welled in her eyes and rolled down her cheeks and splashed onto Luke's face.

When Luke died I wondered, not for the first time: How many losses can you bear? How long before you close down and hope for nothing from the day except to get through it and stay numb?

Chapter Thirty Three

HE DIED EARLY in the day and I was sure they'd run clips of his work on the early news. While I waited for it to begin I found myself remembering a party we'd arranged for one of the times Billy came back from the hospital. Our official version of our childhood had always been that Billy and I never had parties when we were growing up. But I remembered wheedling and nagging at our mother on that occasion and although she didn't tell me in advance that she'd given in, when he came home there was food waiting under clean tea towels in the kitchen. I remembered my amazement, and the shine on Billy's face, when I lifted off the towels and saw the spread of sandwiches and pastries. Our mother told us to serve ourselves lemonade and left the room.

I remembered another time when we'd had to go and see a new caseworker who'd been assigned to our family. Our mother didn't know how to introduce herself, so she fell back on us. "These are my big sons," she said with a fairly shit-eating smile by way of introduction.

"Shortly after Luke Carroll was diagnosed with AIDS over a year ago," the co-anchor said, "he made a tape which he asked us to air if he died of the disease which has killed so many Americans. We at Channel 7 viewed the tape for the first time this afternoon, and we're playing it for you now in its entirety."

"This is Luke Carroll reporting for Channel 7 News." He paused as usual, leaving his mouth open to show his upper teeth.

187

The report had been taped in Luke's apartment. He sat holding a microphone on the old sofa in front of the open glass doors overlooking the garden. Pale winter sun shone across his head and shoulders from a side window. He looked young in an open-necked shirt, and rested.

"I hope that when you see this tape we'll be looking at it together," Luke said, as usual chewing at the words for maximum effect. "Maybe as a historical curiosity dragged out of the vault years from now after we found a cure for AIDS. I hope with all my heart that I survive." Luke's voice broke suddenly and his face crumpled. My heart swelled.

He stopped to regain control, then redirected his usual level and affectionate gaze at the camera.

"More likely, Channel 7 will play this tape the night they announce that Luke Carroll died of AIDS. I was diagnosed in January, and the life expectancy of a middle-class AIDS patient after diagnosis is still just two to three years."

His professionalism took over and he paused automatically to establish sincerity and seriousness of purpose.

"I am only one of an irreplaceable generation that died," Luke said. "Scientists, barbers, doctors, actors, teachers, store clerks, accountants, bathhouse attendants, politicians. It happened that in America most of the first men who contracted AIDS were gay. It was fortunate for America and for the world that AIDS chose to attack some of the strongest and most talented. Because we knew how to fight back. We'd had to learn to survive. We'd had to learn to fight for recognition and freedom to live our lives as we wished when much of the world wanted to see us branded or penalized for asserting our true identity.

"Because we learned to be strong, when AIDS struck we refused to lie down and die. For years we fought an indifferent Washington administration for money for research and treatment. We fought for humane care of those who were already sick, and created our own organizations for loving care of our brothers. Because of our fight, despite the cruel neglect of the media in the early days, more has been learned about AIDS in a shorter time than about any disease in history. Millions of men and women at risk in America and in other countries will benefit from the results of our struggle. Because we *demanded* an unprecedented attack on the disease that was killing us, because the weapons that work against AIDS will work against all disease, humanity will benefit from increased understanding of the diseases that affect everyone."

Pause to indicate the argument is modulating to another level. "It isn't easy knowing that you're probably going to die," Luke said. "But it was never easy being a gay man. I'd like to ask those who still attack us to learn instead to accept us. I learned when I accepted myself as I am that acceptance is a sign of love and strength, not weakness. And we will prevail. Nothing anybody can do can ever kill my brothers, not if every single one of us died tomorrow. Because as long as men and women love each other and create children in their own likeness, with relentless probability they will create endless generations of gay men and women."

Luke reached out of camera range and produced a glass of sparkling wine which he held towards the viewers. "To life," he said, and sipped. "This is Luke Carroll reporting for Channel 7 News." He gazed lovingly into the camera, flashed his teeth, and held the pose for a count of three.

"Luke Carroll, dead at 34," the co-anchor said. "Even in his last report, Luke gave us a great deal to think about."

"He certainly did," her co-anchor said. "Good night, Luke, wherever you are."

I'd been having trouble sleeping and trouble jerking off. The power fantasies weren't working. The night Luke died I desperately needed to sleep, and I reached under the bed for the porno magazines I'd found in Billy's bed the night I arrived. I knew he liked straight porno as well as gay because he'd told me he liked to see straight men fucking. As I pulled out the magazines an older, less glossy, fuzzily-printed magazine drew my attention as it hung by scotch tape from the centerfold of the gay magazine it had been hidden inside. The moment I looked at it I knew why Mar had murdered Billy.

Chapter Thirty Four

BACK DOOR BEAUTIES

Rod likes to satisfy his women's needs by pleasuring their poop chutes. For their part, Sharon and Cindy have been hoping for a man who's willing to experiment. Every woman needs a change now and then from regular twice a day meat and potatoes cunt servicing.

When Rod makes his desires known, Sharon shows her appreciation by tongue teasing Rod's hole plugger, being careful to tantalize it to full attention with tiny tongue flicks while resisting her urge to deep throat the pleasure machine that's soon rock hard. Meanwhile, Cindy prepares Sharon's bunghole with deep tongue lunges, although she can already taste the salty liquids flowing from her friend's body as Sharon imagines the pleasure to come.

"Eat her," Rod commands. "Earn my dick!"

Sharon doesn't need to be told twice. She swings around and buries her head in her friend Cindy's pussy, not an unusual place to find her face. When he sees Sharon's pretty cheeks pushing towards him, the pink pleasure hole pointing provocatively in the direction of his peter, Rod can resist her hungry hole no longer. He rams Sharon's bunghole with one thrust of his thick long meat. Sharon opens her mouth wide, not sure whether to scream with pleasure or pain at the sudden skewering, and almost swallows Cindy's twat.

Rod knows how to ration his fuck machine to make his women grateful for what he gives them. He guns Sharon's second cunt just enough to teach her the meaning of ecstasy. Then it's Cindy's turn. Sharon wants her friend to experience the same deep hole-pleasuring, but she still screams with frustration when Rod suddenly pulls out his big satisfier, leaving her backup hole empty and throbbing.

And so on. All three models were younger when they allowed themselves to be photographed in the sexual activity most likely to spread AIDS, and their bodies were heavier; later they'd had the money for better food. The shabby color reproduction reduced everything, flesh and furniture, to shades of pinkish brown, and coarsened bodies and facial expressions. The three models looked chemically strung out and oblivious. But Rod, making up with lack of inhibition for what he lacked in natural endowment, was Mar sporting a Caligula haircut, and Sharon and Cindy – meticulously simulating overripe ecstasy – were Shannon and Valerie.

Chapter Thirty Five

I WAITED WITH my back to the wall on the long side of a rectangular table in the dining room at Hamburger Marys, making sure I was in full view of the waiters and cooks behind the counter. The lunch hour office workers had already gone. There was a tourist couple at a table by the door, and at the bar the usual small crowd that had found a way of life that allowed them to go drinking in the early afternoon. I'd asked Shannon to tell Mar to meet me at two o'clock. I was early, but more by accident than pressure to bring about an ending. I felt some fear of what might happen in the next hour; I knew it was well outside my range to try to predict how Mar would behave. Mostly I felt drained but calm, because seeking revenge on Mar had lost its urgency for me. I knew nothing could stop it. Most of what was about to happen was already under way, and irreversible.

By 2:15 Mar still hadn't shown up. I'd expected him to be late; trying to play games with people's heads was second nature to him. At almost 2:25 Shannon appeared in the doorway looking rather too harassed.

"Mar has to deal with a crisis at the Dormitory," she said, breathing hard in a white blouse. She discovered a mirror behind my head rather than looking me in the eye. "He asked me to bring you over."

"No way," I said.

She threw up her hands and her voice rose. "He can't get away."

"Tell him I'll be here until three," I said. "I have another appointment later in the afternoon."

"He won't be able to come over," Shannon snapped.

I shrugged. She glared at me and hurried away.

I knew that I was Mar's crisis. He sensed he was in danger, although I'd dispatched the messengers just before I left the house and it was too soon for him to have heard from anyone acting on the contents of the packages.

Mar came through the door at five minutes after three. Shannon followed. He wore a lofty look, she was still urgent. They sat opposite me, both small, but with the carnal charge of people who've displayed their bodies publicly in sexual activity. They'd left themselves open to being easily despised.

"I can only stay five minutes," Mar said, looking a little perturbed, for all the world like just another harassed administrator. "We're having problems with some clients." He scrutinized me, opening himself to finding the best way to deal with whatever was coming. It struck me that he was probably extremely efficient at his work.

"Enjoy it while you can," I said. I handed him a manila envelope.

Mar looked irritated and waited, to make his lack of urgency clear to me, then picked up the envelope and half-pulled out the color photocopy. He showed it briefly to Shannon, then pushed it back to me as if it scarcely concerned him.

But he asked: "Who else has seen this?"

"I sent copies to the *Chronicle* and the *Examiner*, and the gay press, and the network news divisions. A reporter from Channel 7 is interviewing me this afternoon. I also sent copies to the Mayor's office and the Health Department and the police. I told them where I found it, in one place you hadn't searched, and how I believe it's connected to Billy's death."

"That's – " Shannon cried, but Mar shook his head. She stopped.

A waiter came over and they both ordered drinks.

"I also sent them an account of how you're extorting money from dying patients, and how you have a kickback deal with your sister's husband for the money you claim to be giving away. I had trouble working out why you bothered to get involved in that roundabout scheme, apart from putting up a show of generosity and respectability. I suppose you arranged it before you realized how much money you'd be able to extort from patients at the Factory."

The waiter brought their drinks. Mar sat watching me expressionlessly. I imagined his mind sorting through the information I'd fed him, looking for loopholes, calculating probabilities. I was pleased to see that when he reached for his drink his hand was shaking. Shannon picked up her drink, held it to her lips, then changed her mind and threw the contents in my face.

I spat the liquor that had got into my mouth onto the floor and grabbed her napkin to wipe myself. I was laughing out loud. The waiter came and hovered, not quite knowing what to do, and I signalled him to go away.

"Why are you laughing?" Mar asked unwillingly. I knew he hated to admit that he wasn't completely in charge.

"I enjoy the self-righteous indignation of the criminal garbage of the world," I said, turning to Shannon, "when you're found out." Her face was starting to twist in frustration and rage. "It's over," I said to Mar.

He started to speak.

"You may never be charged with Billy's murder," I said, then it occurred to me to put an idea in Shannon's head and I looked at her again. "Unless some of your colleagues decide to make a deal with the prosecution."

"Never," Shannon squawked, hiding her eyes.

"But the city money for the Dormitory will be cut off immediately, no matter who you have on your payroll, and the patients' families won't let them go near the Factory, and you're all going to be under investigation for ever. It's over."

Mar looked tired. He decided something. "I have to get back to the Dormitory," he said, starting to rise.

I reached out and grabbed his hand, which got lost in mine. He sat down and I let go.

"You didn't have to kill Billy," I said. "Someone else was bound to come across a copy of that porno magazine and you couldn't keep killing everyone who found it. You could have lived it down. You could have pleaded ignorance. You didn't know when you were young and poor that you were getting yourselves immortalized in the one sexual activity that's most likely to spread AIDS. My guess is Billy found out you were extorting money from the patients and he threatened you with the magazine to make you stop. But you were scared and too greedy to stop."

"I'll be happy to talk about Billy back at the Dormitory," Mar said.

"Valerie's there," Shannon said, wiping her eyes. "She has something interesting to say to you."

"You people are as interesting as watching a mouse take a shit," I said.

But something happened. Mar was staring at me, something warm in his eyes, and Shannon started looking at me too. Maybe that was enough. I wasn't used to having the attention of even one man or woman concentrated on me like that. Most of the people I knew were recovering drunks who waited for a break to jump in and talk about themselves. Shannon smiled, and for a moment, even that late, they almost convinced me they were my friends. Just getting some attention from someone was almost enough to make me believe anything.

Then I noticed how tight the skin was around Mar's eyes, like the skin on the upper part of Billy's face just after he died. And then the music stopped – I hadn't realized there'd been music playing, but now I retrieved the memory of rock music so loud that in the silence our faces still held traces of the strain of shouting at each other to be heard. If other people hadn't heard us it was because they were shouting too.

I lowered my voice. "I begin to understand the power you people have," I said. "It wasn't necessary to kill Billy."

"We were all that Billy had," Mar said.

"Yes," Shannon echoed.

"Your brother had been killing himself for years," Mar said. "Nothing had worked out for him. He had no friends, no purpose."

Which was true. But it was hard to listen to Mar. His voice had become a crazy salad of accents and his voice had started to race and slow down from one word to the next. He checked himself, glancing at me with hatred that I was hearing this. But I knew I'd beaten him.

He continued, trying to keep his voice together: "He'd been replaying the same scenes in his life like a loop tape in a supermarket. He was lost. We gave him a purpose, and he started to shine. Then like so many people he forgot what we'd done for him and he started to criticize us."

"I've guessed Billy was lost almost since I arrived in San Francisco," I said. "He needed me. He deserved better than you. You're flotsam washed up by the epidemic. You exploited him, and when he found out who you really were you killed him. He was strong enough not to be taken in by you, despite all the pressure. What did you have on Luke Carroll?"

Shannon opened her mouth to protest, virtuous to the last. Mar shook his head and stood up.

"I never seek revenge," he said. "I always recommend forgiveness. One of our clients claimed Luke had unsafe sex with him without telling him he had AIDS. It was supposed to have happened after Luke was diagnosed but while the client was still well. I don't know if it was true. Luke certainly had nothing to fear from me. I wouldn't have revealed the story, and I'd have done my best to prevent the client revealing it. It's history now. The client died a week before Luke. But Luke was always worried about his career." Mar sighed and lifted his chin resolutely. "I really must go now. Are you coming back with us?"

"Which one of you threw Billy out of the car?" I asked. "Who was driving?"

Mar smiled and floated out the door. Shannon followed, walking sideways to make sure I didn't attack him from behind.

I waited, then after a few minutes I followed them.

Chapter Thirty Six

I WAS SO late getting back to the apartment that I thought the TV crew had gotten tired of waiting for me. When I called the station the assignment desk rescheduled me because they'd gone to cover another event in the same story.

"Marlin Golding, the head of a shelter that cared for homeless AIDS patients, fell to his death in a bizarre fire south of Market late this afternoon," the co-anchor announced. "Barbara Zahn has the story."

Cut to Barbara, holding a microphone outside the bread factory next to the archway that led to the Dormitory. "The fire occurred behind this archway," Barbara said, "in the Dormitory, a home for the AIDS homeless that was once a gay bathhouse. Golding apparently jumped off the roof of the four story building, his body in flames. At least five others died inside the former bathhouse, including two staff members, at least one of them a woman, although no other names have been released. The other victims are believed to be AIDS patients, clients of the Dormitory. Firemen had to break down doors locked and barred on the inside. In a bizarre twist, a fireman told me the victims had apparently been involved in a quote *sexual orgy* unquote and may have been using drugs, which might explain why they clung together in a group and did not attempt to escape even the worst of the flames. The bodies were identified by the Dormitory's financial manager, who was away at the time the fire occured. He is now under observation on the psychiatric ward at General

Hospital." Tape of Wink being led away by two paramedics. "This is Barbara Zahn for Channel 7 News."

"In another bizarre twist," the co-anchor said, "on tonight's late news we will hear from a Minneapolis attorney who claims his brother was murdered by Marlin Golding, and the reasons why."

The autopsy revealed that Mar had internal AIDS lesions; Shannon's blood was positive for antibodies to the virus. The Dormitory was gutted. The clients who died were never identified. Sometimes I see Edwin's face in the flames. Sometimes I see Billy's.

As soon as Mar died and they interviewed me again on TV, other reports about Mar's corruption began to appear, including finally a long investigative report in a magazine that had once named Mar, Humanitarian of the Year. I could imagine the glee with which the media published photos of prominent local politicians and gay leaders visiting Mar at the Dormitory. An *Examiner* reporter contracted to write a book about Mar and the Factory and the Dormitory. So far I've turned down her requests for interviews. More patients' families came forward with involved stories about plots to extort money from them; there were accounts of drug abuse and sexual abuse with both clients and volunteers as victims. The maze became a notorious symbol of all the wrongdoing. Apparently Mar had reopened it on special occasions, although that was one of the riskiest things he could have allowed to happen. It was as if he had to test the limits of what he could get away with, see how long he could triumph while he invited disaster.

I still don't understand how he got away with so much for so long. The papers and TV were lazy, as they always are, only reporting the news that other people have already created for them. A lot of people in the AIDS industry were scared of counter-accusations if they rocked the boat. But how could it have happened that it took a half-mad stranger to bring about Mar's downfall? I don't really understand.

Of course he had his defenders who said the good outweighed the bad. Some even attributed a mystical significance to the manner of his death. *People* magazine reported, among other things, that Vincent Mancini, "a freelance microcomputer consultant to large corporations," saw Mar's flaming body pause in the air halfway through its flight down from the roof. "He was still alive, and he was speaking in tongues," Mancini was reported to have said. "I'll remember the sight as long as I live. It's taught me to be careful about believing bad things about anyone."

I think that in terrible times people begin to attribute meaning to events, or create omens, that are in truth as meaningless as the terror itself.

TO RICHARD OLIVER

In Memory

Recent crime from GMP;

Jeremy Beadle
DEATH SCENE

The discovery of Guy Latimer's mutilated body in an alleyway near one of London's leading gay nightclubs opens this intriguing and compulsive first novel. Suspicion for the murder soon falls on Guy's circle of gay friends, all of whom seem to be hiding crucial information, but who find themselves obliged to join forces to try and solve the killing, fearful of a set-up by the police. Death Scene is a highly innovative and cleverly plotted mystery, a classic whodunit firmly placed in London's gay community.

ISBN 0 85449 088 4   Price: £4.95

Rohase Piercy
MY DEAREST HOLMES

These are the recently discovered reminiscences of Dr Watson on his long friendship with the celebrated Sherlock Holmes, which were never intended for publication during their lifetimes. These two new stories throw a fresh light upon their famous partnership, and help to explain much which has puzzled their devotees.

"Thoroughly amusing ... Wonderful stuff" - Stanley Reynolds, The Guardian.

ISBN 0 85449 081 7   Price: £3.95

Joseph Hansen
BACKTRACK

Did Eric Tarr, small-time Hollywood actor, really kill himself? He left behind a lot of broken promises, broken hearts and broken lives. Backtracking through his father's past, young Alan begins to see how many men and women had a motive for murdering him. By the time he learns the truth, it becomes his own personal tragedy, as he waits helpless and defenceless for his father's killer to find and kill him too.

ISBN 0 85449 054 X   Price: £3.95

Chris Hunt
THORNAPPLE

A renegade monk; a scheming lady of the manor; a mysterious old woman and a beautiful boy guarding magical secrets - these are just some of the intriguing characters encountered by a young pedlar as he journeys through the east of England in 1204. Their stories intertwine to form a fast-moving tale of romance, murder and withcraft, taking us from Norman castle to Saxon hovel, from the studios of Paris scholars to the dens of London thieves. Once again Chris Hunt has created a unique work of historical fiction, weaving a rich and imaginative tapestry of people and places to bring the early thirteenth century vividly to life.

Praise for Chris Hunt's previous work:

"The seamless prose and the author's ability to draw parallels between our times never interfere with the pleasure of reading. There are no pretensions to literary snobbery .. though .. what Hunt has done is no less than the finest of literature, creating myth, in its most powerful form, whose vision enriches us" - John Preston.

ISBN 0 85449 104 X   Price: £6.95

Recent titles from GMP:

Kenneth Martin
AUBADE
With a new introduction by the author

Reprinted as a Gay Modern Classic in February 1989, *Aubade* created a storm of controversy with its frank revelations about adolescent homosexual feelings and consciousness when first published in 1957. It tells the story of Paul, a young school leaver, whose life is transformed when he meets a young medical student who he renames 'Gary'. Their relationship develops through the long, hot summer, to reach its climax with the approach of Autumn...

"Not many books by anyone so young are worth publishing, but this was" - John Betjeman.

"Resolves the mixed and complex emotions of adolescence into the timeless purity of art. Most books about such years come from the pressure of emotional memory: Kenneth Martin writes from the very heart of them" - Elizabeth Bowen, Tatler.

"This first novel was not only polished and well-constructed, it was also quite brave for the love that wasn't supposed to dare speak its name to utter forth from a teenager" - City Limits.

"What makes the book remarkable is that the author wrote it at the age of 16. It therefore treats very closely the concerns of adolescents, yet is maturely sophisticated in style and structure" - Sunday Times.

"The book would have been an impressive performance from a mature writer, from a seventeen-year-old tyro it was quite astonishing" - Gay Times.

ISBN 0 85449 097 3   Price: £4.95

Timothy Ireland
THE NOVICE

Romantic and uncertain, Duncan Crowther is 23 years old and still a virgin, drawn to London in his search for love. And from the moment he arrives in the capital, it's clear that whatever happens, his life will never be the same again.

Timothy Ireland's previous novel for GMP *Who Lies Inside* earned considerable praise and won the Other Award for teenage fiction in 1984. *The Novice* develops some of the themes of his earlier work to portray an intimate and disarmingly honest story of innocence and experience, and the hopes and realities of loving and being loved for the first time.

"Ireland's writing reminded me of the gritty, cold-water realism of Alan Sillitoe. He is not the first to use the convention of the unreliable narrator, but few have pulled it off so convincingly. That he succeeds as well as he does heralds a new tremendously talented writer on the gay fiction scene" - San Francisco Sentinel.

"I found *The Novice* wonderfully sincere and felt and fresh ... It's a lovely piece of writing" - Edmund White.

ISBN 0 85449 089 2   Price: £3.95